THE SIXTH HORSEMAN

**Center Point
Large Print**

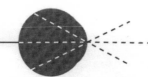

**This Large Print Book carries the
Seal of Approval of N.A.V.H.**

THE SIXTH HORSEMAN

WILLIAM R. COX

Center Point Publishing
Thorndike, Maine

This Center Point Large Print edition
is published in the year 2003 by arrangement with
Golden West Literary Agency.

The text of this Large Print edition is unabridged. In other
aspects, this book may vary from the original edition. Printed in
Thailand. Set in 16-point Times New Roman type by
Bill Coskrey and Gary Socquet.

ISBN 1-58547-276-X

Library of Congress Cataloging-in-Publication Data.

Cox, William Robert, 1901-
    The sixth horseman / William R. Cox.--Center Point large print ed.
    p. cm.
    ISBN 1-58547-276-X (lib. bdg. : alk. paper)
    1. Large type books. I. Title.

PS3553.O9466 S59 2003
813'.54--dc21

2002031520

THERE I WAS, TIMOTHY BRADFORD YOUNGER, fourteen years of age, never had nothin', aint got nothin' and no prospects of nothin'. We did have some sort of dream, us kids. This was in 18 and 91. Benjamin Harrison was President. He was from Ohio, which made him a damyankee but his daddy had been a farmer and farming was respectable and back-breaking and that made it like a religion to till the land. Because everything unpleasant and hateful was good for you. Everybody agreed on that.

Some of us just didn't go along with it. We believed it, all right. Thing was we figured to go to flamin' hell anyways and just didn't worry about it. You take farm kids, they see the animals copulatin' every day, they see the girls bendin' over without underpants, what do you expect? The girls, they left off the underpants as a signal, they were as raunchy as the boys, some of them. They'd help steal a bit of moonshine and creep into the hayloft or out in a sweet smellin' field and in no time at all we were at it. Country kids got it all over city kids that way.

Country folks always had vittles, too. I would've starved if they weren't willin' and able to let me do chores, feed me and sleep me in the barn or some place. They didn't have cash money but they growed their vegetables and killed their meat. And in that country people shared. They was also loyal to their own kind. Smartest thing the Daltons ever did was set up an underground like the James Boys had in Missouri. In the end it fell apart, but then Jesse was shot in the back by a man he had trusted. You can augur and debate but you can't ever make things come out just right. Just about the time you proved the people were loyal they turned around and informed on somebody. It was a wild time, but it's always wild times, seems like. Thing is, are you mixed into it or are you settin' and watchin'?

Another thing you got to remember is that the Border States were full of old hates from the War. People still talked about Jayhawkers and Quantrill, there was mixed feelings always. The War ended in '65 but it never quite got ended in that country. Neighbors hated neighbors too often. Our family was Secesh, and the Daltons took it up although they was too young to have been in it and their papa was a nogood sutler for the Union Army . . . But then Lewis Dalton was no good for anything, ever.

Some of the things I got to tell you I sure didn't know then, in '91, but learned later. But if I put them in the proper place the story will go better, so I will do so. Like Lewis Dalton never was any good but Ma Dalton was. Like there were plenty good Daltons around, some brothers and sisters of the Gang. The Gang was of course Bob, Grat and Emmett. Old Bill, he was in California politickin' when the ridin' and robbin' started. Frank, he was a Marshal in the Territory and he got killed in action, and then Bob became a Marshal outa old Hangin' Judge Parker's district and Bob hired Grat and then the two of them started the shenanigans. Marshalin' didn't pay all that much and was kinda slow payin' anything and the Daltons couldn't abide that so they started things, like stealin' horses from the Indians and such. Which was not too risky if you wore a star.

Of course they were young. Emmett was just a boy, born in 18 and 72. Grat was the oldest, meanest and dumbest. Bob, born in 18 and 70, was the leader. When they picked

6

up with Charlie Bryant and Bitter Creek Newcomb and the others, they just naturally took over. But the real brain, believe me—the one that set things up and provided the cash and all—was the girl named Florence Quick. She called herself a flock of other names in her time, but she was Flo Quick and a nice piece she was too.

Trouble with the Daltons was also that they had Jesse James always in their minds. Jesse this and Jesse that. After the train robbery at Wharton, which made the Daltons famous, they kept sayin' how they were going to do better than Jesse. They got maybe five, six hundred dollars off the train at Wharton and still they thought they could top Jesse. They didn't allow for faster trains, better connections by wire, even telephones here and there. Lordy, Jesse ran around free for sixteen-eighteen years until he got careless, and that was back in 18 and 83. He stole more money on one job than the Daltons put together in the year and a bit more they lasted as robbers.

Anyways, the financial position of Papa Lewis Dalton was always bad. He run fifteen kids outa poor Ma Dalton but he could never make a decent dollar. Most of the time he hung around Coffeyville trying to trade horses. He wasn't a thief, he was just poor white trash and finally the family turned him out. He was about twenty years older'n Ma anyway and took to booze in the end and died miserable and alone. Like anybody else, right? Nobody dies real happy, seems to me.

What I'm gettin' at, the Dalton boys—Bob, Grat, and Emmett—was raised right around Coffeyville. Everybody knew 'em, they had a strong family resemblance—little mouths, little eyes, big ears, you knew they was brothers.

This become very important later on, like I'll tell you. Coffeyville always knew the Dalton boys, could recognize 'em in a flash.

They were not smart. Flo Quick, she was smart, but things always went wrong with the Daltons. You couldn't blame Flo. You had to know it was the fault of the boys and their dumb friends. So much has been told and wrote about the gang, you can look it up. If you had to be around them and see the way they acted and listen to 'em, specially Bob, you would know more, which is what I'm about to tell you. Talk about an empty barrel makin' the loudest noise. And them tryin' to go Jesse one better. They couldn't hold a candle to Jesse's pet pup.

Now me, I was in a little trouble experimentin' with the daughter of a farmer name of Clinton over in Missouri. You got to remember the Border States was all conglomerated together and a body could move across state lines on a walk or by hitchin' a ride in one of the farm wagons. The wagon I got into was going to Coffeyville to market, that being the biggest town around, about 3,500 people.

I had nary a copper. Being always handy with horses, I turned in at a livery stable on Ninth Street near Walnut. A skinny man with a droopy mustache and tiny sharp eyes and eyebrows that curved upward, making him always look a little surprised, was cleaning a rifle. His name was on a sign over the barn.

I said, "Mr. Kloehr?"

"Who wants to know?" He was looking me over sharp with them eyes. I was big for fourteen and strong, but my butternut clothes was shabby and my shoes a mess from scuffin' the road.

"Name of Timothy Younger. I'm lookin' for work. I get along with horses."

"You one of them Youngers, boy?" He sighted the rifle to the weathervane on the barn, which was a horse galloping, only the legs was all wrong, the horse would've killed itself trying to gallop that way.

"Nope. My folk come from Kentucky. They all dead now."

"Don't hold with Youngers or Jameses or Daltons. You related to them Daltons?"

"Nope. Just heard about 'em."

"How old are you, boy?"

"Seventeen." I had to lie about that. Him and his rifle, he was making me nervish. I thought maybe I wouldn't like to work for him after all.

"Can you shoot?"

"Not real good."

"H'mmm." He bent over the rifle like it was a pretty young girl across his lap. "We got a rifle club here. I'm the president. We can outshoot any damn club in the country."

"I can play baseball."

"Ain't interested in the ball club. Just the rifle club. You say you know horses?"

"Raised with 'em."

"Looks to me like you wasn't raised at all, boy. You sure you just wasn't drug up?"

"Well, guess I'll find the man interested in the ball team." I started to turn away.

"Whoa," he said. "Just a minute. A man can't have everything, I've found. I do need a boy."

9

"I ain't askin' much." He seemed friendly now and I was hungry. "If I could get some grub and a place to sleep and a mite to spend."

"I'll pay. I got a bed in the loft. Two dollars a week and I feed you. You put one of the two dollars in the Condon Bank."

"But I need clothes."

He said, "I'll buy you some duds. A boy won't get no place if he don't save. I won't have no shiftless, drunk bum boy around, you understand boy?"

Well, a dollar would buy a lot. I said, "Okay, Mr. Kloehr. You want me to start now?"

"Go into the house. Wash up. Eat. Then you start."

"Thanks, Mr. Kloehr."

"Don't thank me. Just do your job and save your money. Maybe I can teach you to shoot. I'm the champion around here."

He didn't look like any champion to me, a skinny guy with a round hat and those clown eyes and the droopy mustache, but it wasn't any time to augur. I went into the house and they fed me. I was mighty hungry. I ate pork chops and corn on the cob and taters and sorghum molasses on biscuits—they fed good—until I was like to bust. Then I went back to the barn, about staggerin' under the load of vittles.

The work was light, just cleanin' stalls, saddlin' and hitchin' up for them that rented horses, feedin' and handlin' the straw and such. I liked the smell of horse manure, like ammonia. The beasts understood me and let me curry and comb them, and I always had 'em lookin' sharp. Mr. Kloehr didn't pay much attention except to collect the fees. He was always foolin' around with one or another of his rifles, the Remington or the Winchester. He kept them in beautiful condition. And he could shoot—man how he could shoot. He could beat anybody. Not with pistols—he hadn't any use for pistols—just long guns.

He was a fair man. He bought me decent clothes and paid on the spot and made sure I put the dollar in the Condon Bank, which was on Walnut Street right opposite the First National Bank. I got to know a real important man, one of the co-owners, Mr. Carpenter, and the cashier, Mr. Ball. And young Tom Babb, he worked there off and on, he got me on the ball team. Mr. Kloehr would let me off on Saturday sometimes to play ball, although the weekends was the busiest time at the Livery Stable.

Mr. Ball and Tom was big fans of the Chicago White Stockings of them days. That was a great team—Cap Anson, King Kelly and an outfielder named Billy Sunday, who became an evangelist later and a good player in his time. We read about 'em in the Coffeyville *Journal* and tried to do things the way they did. Somehow the inside tricks didn't work so good for us but we had a pretty good team, Lucius Baldwin and a bunch of other young fellas. I was the youngest but they didn't know it. A big fan of ours was Carey Seaman, a funny lookin' little barber, one of Kloehr's rifle club people. Carey wanted to play but he couldn't catch and he couldn't hit. He was just a fan.

Coffeyville had a lawman, Marshal Charles T. Connelly, who should've been a preacher. He always forgot to carry his revolver. The town had been a hellhole in the earlier days, but by 18 and 91 it had quieted down until all Connelly had to do was take care of drunks. He was a gentle kind of man, everybody liked him, but he shouldn't ever have been a law officer.

It was a nice town for that day and time but the trouble was they had cleaned it up too good. The businessmen and the church people had got a mortal lock on Coffeyville. Outside of baseball and church socials and a picnic now and then, what was there to do? Unless you was on the rifle team—then you got a lot of action practicin' and all that. I tried because Mr. Kloehr wanted me to but I was never any great shakes with a rifle. Funny thing, I could shoot offhand with a pistol real good, but nobody cared about that in Coffeyville.

And there wasn't any girls. I mean there wasn't any for me, a stranger and a stablehand with no family, nothin'. Nobody invited me to stand around a piano and sing along. Furthermore they had closed down the whorehouses. I would've been willing to spend my dollar just to see inside of one but they had shut them down tight. That's why I was took in so easy.

She come drivin' into the livery stable in a dusty buggy. The horse, a ratty chestnut, had a loose shoe. This was in August and it was a sultry day. She wore a light plaid dress open at the neck and boots on her tiny feet. She was a little lady with a round face and wide eyes and the prettiest skin and her hair was pulled up on top and drawn back and she wore a perky bonnet and she smiled, although she was tired and unhappy about the horse and hungry and a whole lot of other things.

She said her name was "Mrs. Pierce," but she didn't wear any wedding ring so I figured she was either divorced or a widow. There was something about her that told you she was free. Not that she didn't look nice and ladylike and all that. It was in her eyes, the way she smiled, the way she looked at you up and down. It was in her manner, real brisk and businesslike even when she was smiling. She didn't say where she came from nor where she was going, just could she get the horseshoe fixed and put up the rig. Mr. Kloehr didn't pay much attention; he was cleaning his guns again.

I said, "Yes, ma'am, I can fix the shoe. Fifty cents to board the horse and another fifty for feed. Unless you aim to stay awhile, then it's on a weekly rate."

She asked, "Are you Mr. Kloehr's son?"

"No ma'am. Name of Timothy Younger."

She gave me a quick, knowing look as if all of a sudden we understood one another, and by gun it was that way. We did understand each other right then and there. She walked over to the horse, lifted the right foreleg and touched the pastern, which was swollen.

"See, it's a day or so rest for him, wouldn't you say?"

I had to lean close to her. She handled the horse so you knew what she was doing. She was bent half over and I could smell her and the hot day made the dress cling tight to her bosom and I could see the nipples. She turned her head so that she was talking in my ear and she whispered.

"I'm real short of cash. Could you manage it for me?"

"I ain't got much. I'd have to pay him—Kloehr."

"You're a Younger. Kin to the Daltons. I'm a friend of the Daltons."

I didn't say I was no kin. With her leaning against me a little and breathin' in my ear I woulda been kin to the Devil long as she wanted it that way.

I said, "I'll manage it."

She said, "Just one or two days."

"I can handle it."

She straightened up and said so Kloehr could hear, "I'll be at the hotel. Come and tell me what you think."

"Yes'm," I said. "After supper."

"That'll be fine."

She didn't ask where the hotel was located so I figured she knew the town. I watched her go. She had a swing to her hips. She'd been married, or something, all right. Even at my age, then it was easy to tell. Kloehr never looked up from his guns as I unhitched the horse and took him in the stable and put him in a stall and gave him some extra feed and got a nail and a hammer and clinched the shoe. He was lame but not real sore. He was a parrot mouth nogood but he seemed sound enough. I wiped him down and gave him some straw for a bed and went about my other chores.

It was an afternoon as long as I can ever remember. You got to know us country lads was doin' it since we was twelve and we missed it when we didn't get and I hadn't had none in a long time. Now I knew as good as anything I was goin' to get it. Further and more I was goin' to pay for it just like in a regular house and that sorta added to the thrill. I mean you wouldn't have to fight for it or nothin'. You was makin' a deal. It was yours, like you bought anything else. To a boy that was somethin' extra and fine. Took away all the guilty feeling.

When I had ate I washed good in the barn with the hose and some soap Tom Babb had given me, smelled good. I put on the new clothes—hadn't worn 'em more'n a few times—and went around to Walnut Street and slipped in the back way of the hotel. I knew the nigra chore boy pretty good and he looked surprised but didn't say nothin', and he wouldn't because I showed him a fist and shook my head. I asked him in what room the lady was and he told me and I still remember, Number 23 on the second floor in the back, a cheap room. So I believed her, she didn't have much money to spend.

I went up them stairs quiet and slinky as a tomcat on a back fence. If I told you I wasn't breathin' hard and shakin' at the knees I'd be a liar. This was a growed lady and all I had knowed was country gals seldom more'n a year older then me. The funny thing was I was surer of this lady than I ever was of one of the country gals. It was somethin' you couldn't help knowin', that was the way she was.

When I got to the head of the stairs there she was. I flattened myself against the wall. She was talking to a drummer I had seen about town. He shook his head and went down the front way. I came away from the wall and walked toward her. It was night by now and there was only a wall lamp which flickered. She saw me and her face changed and she smiled real nice. She opened the door to Number 23, and I followed her inside. It was a little room with scarcely room for an iron bedstead and a dresser. It didn't have a closet, just hooks on the wall behind a curtain. There was a water pitcher and a basin and a pot sticking under the bed and a window which she had left open to get some air. The shade flapped and she didn't light the lamp. We sat on the edge of the bed.

I took out my dollar and said, "This'll do for one day feed and storage." I wanted her to see I had the real dinero.

"I knew you would." She talked in a whisper like at the livery stable. She had a Texas lingo, sort of, mixed up with other soft ways of talking. She took the dollar and put it on the wash stand. She said, "So you're a Younger."

"Timothy Younger."

"Timothy. Yes. You know about horses, I can tell."

"Yes'm." I wasn't interested in horses. We were about two feet apart on the edge of the bed. I couldn't see her so plain, but there she was.

"You know about the Daltons, too."

"Sure. Everybody knows about the Daltons now."

"What do you think?"

"Anybody robbin' a railroad is okay with me. Railroads is ruinin' the horse business." That's what a lot of men were saying so I just repeated it. Mr. Grump the drayman was always moanin' that the railways were puttin' him out of business. Besides, she'd told me she was a friend of the Daltons and I wasn't about to go against anything she liked, not at that moment.

She said, "The Daltons need horses. Good horses."

"Well, the way I hear it, they know where to come by 'em. Down in the Territory?"

"There are too many lawmen looking for the Daltons. They can't move around good."

"Guess that's right." It was still too hot and I had on a coat. I didn't have the nerve to take it off.

She said, "I'd sure like to get the boys some fast horses."

"You? A lady?"

"It's better for me. I can get places they can't."

"You must be a real good friend of theirs."

"Yes. I am." She laughed a little and moved on the bed and then she was closer to me and I didn't know whether it was hot or cold or what as she took hold of my hand. "You sure are big and strong. How old are you?"

"Eighteen." I figured I might as well add another year.

"My, I would have said you were at least twenty-one. Is your family here in town?"

"I ain't got any family." I was squeezing her hand. It was getting so I didn't know if I could wait much longer.

"No family at all?"

"None. I live over the livery stable."

"Then there's nothing to keep you in Coffeyville?"

"Well . . . no, reckon not."

"You don't have a steady girl?"

"Nope."

"It must be lonesome for you." She squeezed my hand back and leaned against me. For a little lady she sure had big bosoms.

"It sure is." I got one arm around her. She felt soft and cuddly. I tried to kiss her and managed to hit her nose. She laughed a little, very soft.

"Come on, honey, we can do better than that."

She turned my head around and give me the first real kiss ever. It was so warm and wet and it lasted so long I thought I would bust. In fact I did bust.

I couldn't hold it any longer.

She knew it right away and she was all concern. She fussed and blamed herself and to tell the truth I could've slugged her. But she made me take off my clothes and she went to the basin and washed my pants and all and then she hung them up and cooed at me like a turtle dove and took off her clothes. She wasn't wearing as many as other ladies I had observed. She lay down on the bed and pulled me alongside her and whispered in my ear.

"Don't you fret, honey. You just lay here with Kate

17

awhile and it'll be fine. I've seen enough to know how fine it'll be. Kate just loves a man with a big one. You just stay here and we'll show them something."

That's the first I heard her name was Kate, but it didn't matter none after a few minutes. One thing about a boy between twelve and eighteen, he can waste one any time and come back for more. Yessir, Kate knew more tricks than a monkey on a stick. That first time it went so fast and my head was so whirly I didn't appreciate half them tricks. Later on I did, and all my life I been grateful to her. She sure did not spare herself. She was right there, nine ways to the gun.

When we was finally worn completely out the sky was beginning to get light. Reckon we'd slept a little betwixt times. It was all a big dream come true to me.

She said, "Timothy you are great."

"You some punkins yourself," I told her.

"What a night."

"The mornin' was pretty good, too."

She laughed and kissed me on the neck. Then she said, "Timothy, a man like you can't be satisfied with Coffey-ville."

"Well, I got plans, of course." I didn't have nary a plan in the world, not even how to get back into the stable without being seen and having the strength to do the chores.

She said, "Timothy, I know where there's some horses."

"Well, sure. Everybody's got horses in this country."

"No, I mean over in Oklahoma."

"Yes, but you ain't got any money."

"If I had a man to help I wouldn't need money."

Well, I can't say it was a surprise. Her talkin' so much about the Daltons and all. I didn't say anything for a minute.

All of us had been brought up on stories of the Border Wars and the James Boys and the Younger Brothers, and she figured I was related. Although the Youngers and the Jameses never was related—that's one of them stories, too.

She said, "We could drive to where they are. I've got enough to feed us a few days. We could sleep somehow or other. You wouldn't mind that, would you?"

That was somethin' I sure wouldn't mind, that sleepin' matter. "I got about twelve dollars in the bank."

She said, "We could pay the livery stable, get your money and just drive out."

It wasn't anything to think on a lot, layin' there naked alongside a lady like her, thinkin' about some more of that stuff along the way. And then the Daltons—the more I thought about ridin' free on a fine horse, robbin' trains which was the natural enemy of the people, the more I cottoned to the notion.

I said, "Tom Babb can get my money. If we pay Mr. Kloehr, then I don't owe nobody anything. Wouldn't want to cheat people that've been good to me."

"Of course not. Never cheat the people. Only the railroads. That's right and proper."

My clothing was dry by then. We made plans and I stole out of there feelin' more like a tomcat than ever. The nigra saw me and his eyes bugged out, him figurin' easy what I had been doing all night. I ran to the livery stable. I got into the loft without being seen and slept some, but not much because here came Kate. The horse was still a little lame, but not bad. She paid Mr. Kloehr and drove down to the alley behind the stable. I sneaked out the back way and went to the bank and Tom Babb gave me my money and I told him I was taking a trip and he wished me luck and then I got into the buggy and away we went, slow but sure.

We got about eight miles out of town and came to a pasture. It was the Stapleton farm. There was a horse in the field, a chestnut like the one we was drivin', not much more of a nag but it wasn't lame. Kate pulled over.

"Now that would be an even swap," she said.

"You meant steal Stapleton's horse?"

"Not steal it. Exchange ours for it." She laughed and leaned against me with those big boobies. "No harm done, Timothy. One's about as good as the other."

I don't know what would've happened if Stapleton had happened along, but he didn't. I got his horse hitched and turned ours into the field and away we went. Stapleton's chestnut had a lot of bottom and had been standing and was frisky so I took the reins, although Kate could handle them as good as any man. There was a lot of things she could do as good as a man.

We slept in a haymow that night.

The next day she let me buy some food that we could pack along, bread and tins and some jelly and bottles of sass and stuff. We found another haymow at noon. She didn't ever seem to get tired of it, and naturally it interested me a whole lot more than the food. We ate to keep up our strength. We spent a whole week at it. Best week I ever spent in my life.

When we finally come to the place where the horses was it became different. This was a horse ranch, with cowboys and all. Most of them came up from Texas and wore pistols in holsters attached to cartridge belts and they were wanted by the law or they couldn't hold jobs because of booze or they were just plain out-of-work drifters. Invention of the refrigerator cars back in the early '80s and the coming of the rails cut down the number of cowboys needed in Texas. There was no more drives to Kansas after four railroads come to Fort Worth—the city where the drives once began, where the ranchers combined their herds for the trek north, the Cowboy Capital Of The World. It all added up that these cowboys working this Oklahoma horse and cattle ranch called the O-Bar-Z felt like they were the last of a breed and they had to live up to all the hiyu tales of the Man On A Horse, as some writer kept callin' them.

But what I seen was a bunch of stove-up riders with hands full of sores from the ropes and half of them with the old rall and braggin' about it at that and drunk and mean as snakes any time they could steal a bottle of shine. I'd seen 'em in Missouri and Kansas, and now here we were in Oklahoma and it didn't figure to be any different. But Kate was always cautious—she insisted we camp two miles east of the nearest O-Bar-Z pasture and rehearse what we was goin' to do. The campin' part was all right. It was on a little lake or pond she knew about—Kate always knew the dangedest odd things and places—and where we got our first all-over bath that week and then rolled up naked in our blankets for a while. Then it was dark and we had another bath, and then she got real serious, and Kate could do that even standin' in water only to her knees, with those big boobies and that black triangle of hair and all reachin' out and grabbin' at you but her talkin' low and serious like she was in school wearin' a neck-to-ankles Mother Hubbard kind of dress. Like a teacher, she was, and me a dumb scholar.

"Fun's over," she said. "Time to get down to business."

"Aw, just once more?"

"Not even a kiss," she told me. She walked up on the bank and dried herself.

I dove back in and swam awhile to cool myself off. A kid that age don't quite believe everything but he knows a change in the tone of voice, an attitude. It was like she had soused me with scraped ice. It was the first time I really recognized she was a lot older than me. When I came out of the water she was digging into a satchel in the back of the buggy, the one we had not touched before. It was just an ordinary brown bag but she had been mighty tetchy about it, not letting me handle it or anything.

I put on my butternuts, the new ones, and she watched me light a lantern and begin making a fire. We had cold food, but even in August it could get cool lakeside and a fire was friendly. She had put on a grey, long dress with a high collar and her hair was up and she could have been a schoolteacher at that. We sat on a blanket and ate and then buried the tins and whatever was left over.

She said, "You know the Gyp Hills?"

"The Gloss Mountains? No, I never been there."

"Well, they're south of here on the South Canadian."

"I know that much. Riley's ranch is thereabouts. Riley's got a bad reputation. Don't he hire a lot of those Texan cowboys?"

"Riley's a friend," she said.

"Is that where we're headin'?"

"Riley hires all kinds of people but he minds his own business. Now this man that owns O-Bar-Z, he is no friend of Riley's. He hires men who don't cotton to the men Riley hires. You understand that?"

"I ain't dumb. Riley and O-Bar-Z has a feud. Friends of Riley's can steal horses from O-Bar-Z—if they can drive the horses they steal to the South Canadian without gettin' hung or shot."

"You are smart," she said. "You grab on quick. O-Bar-Z is owned by a man named Semple. His foreman is a bit thug named Irish Casey. Neither Riley nor the Daltons got any use for any O-Bar-Z people."

"And the Daltons need horses."

"O-Bar-Z horses. Semple's bred the fastest, toughest ponies in this part of the country."

"Okay. What do we do about it?"

"We need a small bunch, maybe a dozen head."

"And we're supposed to take 'em under the nose of all them tough Texans and all?"

"Timothy, there are ways and means. And still other devices," she said. It was amazin' how she could talk all sorts of ways, down to language you wouldn't believe in the blankets and up to this kind of talkin'. She was all school-teacher now. "The Daltons need horses. They have a plan. We are friends, we can move about without the law on our backs. Don't you see that it is up to us to deliver the horses?"

"If you say it, I see it. But how we're goin' to do it, that's another matter. I never stole nothin' in my life, much less a dozen head of horses."

"Inexperience is an asset in this case," she told me. "We are going to drive to the O-Bar-Z tonight. We will be caught at dark without lodging. You are a pupil, I am a teacher taking you to another school."

"Me, big as I am, a school kid?"

"You will wear your good jacket but your old pants

which are too short for you." She dug into that brown satchel and took out a round, flat-topped boy's hat. "You'll wear this. You'll also try and look simple. I don't mean like an idiot, I just mean young and innocent."

"Kate, I ain't been innocent for a long time. I hardly know how to look thataway."

She gave me a little grin which was like the times in the past week when we had been getting ready to do it, and that made me feel better. Truth is, no matter what I said there was no way to stop me from doin' whatever she suggested. Kate had ways about her nobody could resist. When she put herself onto something she could lead an army.

"Just be yourself and stay behind my skirts," she said. "They won't be looking at you much of the time."

"I can believe that. They'll be lookin' at you."

"And listening to me. They'll believe what I want them to believe. They'll put us up for the night—what else can they do, two strangers lost in the night?"

"But what good'll that do?"

"The horses we want are right where we want them. What we need to know is how many herders are there? Do they watch close or have they got a line camp where the cowboys play cards and loaf and sleep during the early hours of the morning? People are inclined to be slow and sluggish in the predawn hours. That's when patients in hospitals die. Resistance is low, the pulse sluggish. That's when we will be wide awake."

"But Kate I can't drive twelve high-spirited nags into the Gloss Mountains alone. That's a job for two or three good men."

"Two," she said. "You and me."

24

"You're goin' to ride herd?"

"You can bet your last copper on it."

Like I say, you had to believe her. So I said, "Well, all right. But supposin' they chase us and get close?"

"We let 'em come close." She went into that bag again. Now she produced two oiled rags and unrolled them and there was two Colt six-shooters. She put two boxes of cartridges alongside them. "The guns come from the Daltons. The bullets I picked up while you were buying canned peaches the other day."

I remembered how the storekeeper had to get the peaches off in a dark corner and she had been behind me and I thought she made a move or two but I hadn't been any more suspicious than the owner of the place. I was worried because the last dollar of my original ten was all I had and she didn't seem to have any more dinero neither. The two guns glittered dull and ugly in the light of the lantern, yet there was a fascination to them. I picked one up and broke it and saw it wasn't loaded. I looked at her.

"I'm pretty good with one of these here."

"Let's hope we don't have to use them," she said. "But if we do there is only one rule: When you draw, shoot to kill."

She said it offhand, like it was just somethin' a teacher would explain to a pupil. But it gave me the shivers. I was learnin' fast that you can diddle in the bed with a woman for ever so long and still not know all about her. Right now she was a person that I didn't cotton to so awful much. I mean she was cold and sorta deadly and full of herself and her plans. It was like someone had stepped on my grave.

"I ain't about to take a man's life over a few head of horses," I told her.

"Timothy, you don't know what you'll do when someone starts shooting at you."

Well, she had me there. In those days in that country there was first and last a lot of shootin'. I'd heard talk that back even beyond then Coffeyville had its man for breakfast many a day. They had also hanged a woman for murderin' customers that came to her inn outside of town. The woman's name had been Bender. Kate Bender.

She went on, "There's some things you ought to know, Timothy. Once I tell you, there's no turning back—you're one of us, you know that."

"Us? You mean the Daltons?"

"That's right. The Daltons. Bob and Emmett. Bill's around politicking. Grat's on the dodge. You'll meet Big Creek Newcomb and Bill Doolin and Bill Powers and Dick Broadwell. You know what happened to Charlie Pierce."

"Ed Short got him—and got killed doin' it."

"Yes. And me, I'm not Charlie's sister, nor his widow. I'm not Eugenia Moore, although some people think I am. My name is Florence Quick."

Now I did stare and my head did a spin and I shook all over worse than ever. "You're Flo Quick? The way I hear it, Flo Quick is Bob Dalton's gal."

"That's what they say." She was as cool as a cucumber.

"But you . . . me . . ."

"What Bob doesn't know won't hurt him. Besides, he is not what you call the faithful type. Emmett now, him and his Julia, that's another matter. Emmett's young but he's in love with Julia." There was an odd tone to her voice, as though she was not altogether sure of herself for once nor altogether happy. Her eyes were hidden. She touched one of the revolvers as if it gave her strength. "You just mind your manners from now on. You understand?"

"I understand it but I don't like it."

"You'll find other girls."

"Nobody like you," I told her, and she softened again and winked and was smiling as though it was all a good joke between us.

"I do thank you, Timothy. I doubt what you say but I am grateful. I must say you learn fast."

So she knew all the time I was not eighteen and that I didn't know much about girls except bam, bam, thank you ma'am like a rabbit, before her. At the time it didn't bother me. We had entered into a sort of bargain. She had given me something and I was to repay her. It seemed right and natural.

She said, "Bob is the leader, make no doubt about that. Bill Dalton is supposed to be clear of his brothers. He works the towns. He keeps us informed. He is smart but he has a big opinion of himself."

"They say he's into politics up to his neck."

"But not up to his brains. He will never win an election. He tried in California and almost went to jail."

"Grattan Dalton did go to prison, didn't he?"

"He did, the big dummy. And escaped and rode two thousand miles to get back to his brothers. Grat never did have any sense and he drinks too much and he's a worriment. But the Daltons stick together." She shook her head. "Grat's hiding out and I wish he'd stay hidden."

"What about the others?"

"The two Bills . . . Doolin doesn't trust the Daltons but hasn't got the gumption to leave them. Powers is also not

27

clever but he's game. Newcomb is a lost soul but a rider who goes along. Dick Broadwell comes from a good family, like the Daltons. There are good Broadwells and good Daltons all over the Border States, if you call ploughing and starving and going to church being a good person."

"And dyin' a little."

"Right. Anyway, that's the gang. Jim Riley's place is so big and so tangled they built a hideout there in the hills where the river runs, and there they are. Waiting for good horses."

"You said they had plans."

"I've got plans."

"You have?"

"I have my ways. I bring information, then Bob thinks about it. Then they ride."

"I see." It had come gradually so I wasn't scared or anything, nor surprised, neither. Anyone could see how smart she was. There was a whole hell of a lot of people that thought highly of the Daltons, almost as many as thought the other way. So she was one of them. It was all right with me. I never had nothin' and this might be a chance to get somethin'.

She was talking half to herself now. "We've got the organization. It's somewhat like the James Boys and the Younger Brothers had. But you know all about that from your family."

I still didn't say anything. Let 'em believe.

"If only Bob wouldn't be so wrapped up in Jesse and that bunch. Things are so different. A gang can't stay in the country and hide out forever." It was her cross to bear, this fear of being captured. "I keep telling him, one big haul and then we go south across the border. It's the only way."

"To Mexico?"

"Of course. Land is cheap, there are haciendas for sale. Money will buy anything. Anything at all. Mexicans don't ask where it came from as long as it's negotiable. It's the only possible way to stay alive and live decent."

Well, she was right. Later it was Butch Cassidy and the Sundance Kid who went south, but they went to Venezuela and couldn't stop robbin' and killin' and wound up shot to pieces by the army down there. In the nineties it was best to go to Mexico and dig in and become citizens if you had the money. Why there was Confederate veterans down there raisin' families, men that refused to surrender and made it across the line. A couple long riders had made it, but even now I wouldn't mention their names. Ozark people know more'n they ever dare tell.

She said, "Well, you'll learn a lot more. But now we're going to visit Hi Semple."

"Does he know you?"

"If he did I wouldn't be on this dodge," she said. "If I get to be known I won't be any use at all. Now remember, I'm Miss Pierce, a teacher moving to Oklahoma, and you're escorting me down there to go to school and stay with your uncle. Your name is—let me see. Your name is Sammy Parker."

"Parker? You ain't makin' me related to that hangin' judge?"

"Let them think what they may. Just so they don't know who we really are. And don't speak up. Act shy."

"I can do that. On account of I'm scared."

"Everyone is scared first time out." She was loading the

pistols, doing it neat and correct like she did everything, five chambers full, the hammer down on the empty. It sure was funny to see her tiny hands at the job. She put them back in the satchel but she didn't latch up, leaving it so that a gun could be grabbed out in one motion. She put the bag on the floor between us and dropped a kerchief over it to cover up the contents.

I hitched up Stapleton's horse and doused the lantern and hung it underneath the buggy, and she took the reins and drove up the road to the O-Bar-Z. She talked all the way, coachin' me, and the more she talked the more she was the schoolteacher. She should've gone on the stage, that one. She could play any part and do it up brown. She was some woman.

We came to the road leadin' into the ranch house, and I opened the gate and then closed it behind us. There was a bit of a moon and we could see the way. When we pulled up it was about ten o'clock and there was only one light, in the kitchen where people usually stayed to talk or whatever at night. We both went up to the door and a dog barked and Flo—to use her real name, which I always did after this time—gave a little cry like she was scared and Hi Semple himself opened up, a big man with a big nose and a big fat belly. I got behind Flo and tried to act shy but I reckon it was more like dumb.

She said, "Excuse me, sir, but we find ourselves without lodgings for the night. We were given wrong directions somehow or other and misjudged the distance to the next town."

He asked, "Who's that with you, Miss?"

Then I saw he was holding a rifle half behind him. I sort

of gulped as she answered him.

"Why, this is a boy I am taking to his uncle down near Fort Smith. Sammy Parker. I am Miss Pierce. I teach school."

She gave him a gentle smile. He tried to hide the gun, it seeming foolish to hold it on a lady and a boy. He stepped aside and we went into the big kitchen. A skinny Irishman— he had the map on his mug—was sitting at the table with a bottle of whiskey in front of him. He was half drunk.

"This here is my foreman, Casey," said Semple. "Better get to the bunkhouse, Irish, you had enough."

"I never had enough," said Casey. "I had too much and too little. But never enough. Pardon my blather, Miss. I bid you all good night."

He took the bottle with him. Semple scowled after him. You could see the rancher tryin' to haul himself together and show what a gent he was. The booze hadn't affected him as much as it had Casey but he smelled of it to high heaven.

He said, "Ma'am, I got a spare bedroom. If you don't mind. I mean the boy—I got no place for him."

"Oh, Sammy can sleep in the bunkhouse," she said. "I know I can trust you, Mr. Semple. I've heard all about you, how kind you are."

He just purely beamed. "Mighty proud, Miss. Can I rustle you some grub?"

"No, thanks. We ate on the road. Coffee, perhaps?" She sat at the table with her back straight, hands folded prim, all wide-eyed innocence. It was a sight to see. I shuffled to a corner and sort of scrooched to make myself look smaller. There was a pot on the stove and Semple poured and it was blacker than your hat. "Not for Sammy. He's a bit too young for coffee," she said.

31

"I got milk."

He went into the cool room off the kitchen and she whispered, "Find out how many men are on the place. Don't go to sleep. Pump that Irishman—he's drunk already, he'll talk."

Semple came with the milk and I drank it and she told him all about teaching and what a holy profession it was and how she enjoyed the children and all that crap. It wasn't often he had the chance to play the gent and he sure rose to it. You'd have thought she was some saint that dropped in on him out of heaven, the way he treated her.

In just a few minutes I began yawning and rubbin' my eyes and Semple showed me the way to the bunkhouse in back. She give me one little wink behind his back and it was enough to boost my spirits and give me enough juice to go on with it.

The whole thing was crazy if I stopped to think, but on account of her I didn't stop. I went into the bunkhouse and there was a dozen bunks and saddles hangin' up in a corner where they didn't belong, so them must've been personal property of the men, and gunbelts all over and Casey at a table again with his bottle and three men asleep and one sittin' with the Irisher. I stopped inside the door, still trying to look like the country bumpkin.

Casey said, "Come on in, son. Guess you'll be bunkin' in here. There's an empty over yonder."

The other man had long hair and round, protuberatin' blue eyes. He stared at me. Then I saw a badge on his vest. I must've showed how scared I was because he beckoned to me to come into the light of the lamp.

"Who are you, boy?"

Casey answered, "He come in with a lady school-teacher. He's just a dumb kid."

"The Daltons use dumb kids. And all kinds of people," said this fellow. I could see his badge was Federal and he was a deputy. "You know who I am, boy?"

"No, sir."

"I'm Marshal Ransom Payne."

"Yes, sir."

"I been on the trail of the Daltons since they began their depredatin' and stealin' and rustlin'. The day will come when I see them hangin' down at Fort Smith."

"Yes, SIR." He wanted me to either be scared to death or agree with him, so I agreed. "That'll be a fine day."

"I almost had 'em at Wharton."

He had been on the train at Wharton when the Daltons held it up and he had ducked into the weeds and stayed there until it was all over. He was a four-flusher and a phoney but he was here at the O-Bar-Z on the night Flo Quick intended to steal horses and it didn't set well, believe me.

I said, "Do tell," and let my mouth hang open in admiration.

Casey took a drink. One of his eyes drooped. He said, "We hear they hang out up at Jim Riley's ranch. You looked around there, Payne?"

"Took a posse through the whole place. They're not up there. They move around and people protect them." He fixed me with those starey eyes. "You know any people who protect the Daltons, boy?"

"Oh, no sir. I don't know nothin'. I'm only fourteen years old."

"You're damn big for fourteen."

"I know. They say maybe that's why I'm so slow. Growed too fast, they say."

Payne poured himself a drink in a tin cup. "Well, everybody can't be lucky. Now you take my job, Federal Marshal. A man's got to be smart and swift to hold down a job like that."

Casey said, "Deputy Federal Marshal, ain't it, Payne?"

"Just a matter of time." He waved a lordly hand. "Once I bring in the Daltons there'll be a promotion. Maybe up north in a big district. I got ambitions."

"But you don't know where the Daltons hide out."

"If it wasn't for the people. The people protect 'em. I keep tellin' them in headquarters. They oughta hang a few of the friends of the Daltons, that'd bring 'em in."

"Hang people? You mean farmers, storekeepers, like that? Just because they're supposed to be friends of the Daltons?"

"That's what I said."

Casey tipped the bottle, then said, "Well, you asked your questions, Payne. Me and the boys answered 'em. You satisfied we ain't friends of the Daltons?"

"A detective ain't never satisfied complete. But youall seemed okay."

"You're certain of that?"

"Like I say, you seem okay."

"Then why don't you drag your ass outa here?" asked Casey. "The Daltons run with Jim Riley and I'd as soon be Protestant as have anything to do with Riley, the stinkin' Orangeman. But you give me a big pain, Payne."

"Now see here, Casey. Your boss will hear about this. You can't talk to a Federal Marshal like that."

"Deputy Marshal," said Casey again. He made a flashy

34

move and, drunk as he was, he produced a gun pointed at Payne. "You want to make somethin' out of it, Deputy Marshal?"

Payne turned green in the lamplight. He stuttered and he stammered and he knocked over his chair getting away from the table. He didn't say a word anyone could understand as he flew out the door. Casey put the gun away.

"Some lawman," Casey said to me. He yawned and drank again. "Main thing, he was usin' up me whiskey along with his brag. You sleepy, boy?"

"Yes, sir."

"Well, go on and hit the blankets. One more swig and I'll be dead for the night. Got my gut full of big talk." He suddenly began to mumble, counting on his fingers. "Lemme see . . . two men up north pasture. One down south . . . but who cares . . . whattahell? The boss in there with the schoolmarm, let him worry."

I went to the empty bunk and took off my boots and lay down. Casey kept mumbling, finished the bottle. Then he made three attempts before he got the light blowed out. Then he staggered to a door and went through it and closed it and I knew that was his private sleeping place, him being the foreman.

It was hard to stay awake. I heard a horse gallop off and figured that was Marshal Ransom Payne. There was no room for him in the main house anyway and Casey sure had scared him. I thought about being a Marshal and behavin' like Payne, and that took up my mind. Ed Short hadn't been any bargain, neither—a tough man but dumb enough to let Charlie Pierce get hold of a gun when he had

Charlie manacled. There was Chris Madsen and Bud Ledebetter and Heck Thomas and I heard a lot about Bill Tilghman, but mainly the Marshals, Federal or otherwise, were a bunch of skates. Being with the Daltons couldn't be any worse than being with a bunch of cowardly grafters. At least that's what I told myself.

And then I thought how I knew more about Florence Quick than anyone, for she had been a ghost word in the mouths of the people of the Border States, a phantom lady who was only known as the girl friend of Bob Dalton. She had judged me real good. She knew if she confided in me I would never peach on her. The whole training of us people in that place was not to peach. Even if we knew about outlaws we didn't run to the law, Ransom Payne had been right enough about that. This came down from the Border troubles which folks settled among themselves one way or another, sometimes wrong and sometimes right. Way I see it, the law bein' what it is and was, the average was about the same—mistakes will be made because people is people. People is a critter and you can depend on it and not count too much on the blind lady and the scales. I known a few crooked scales in my time.

So I managed to keep awake and was ready when the light little tap come at the door. I put my boots back on and crept out and there she was. And she had changed clothes again—she was the damnedest woman for always havin' different costumes hid out. Now she wore men's britches and boots and a dark shirt and a hat which hid her hair and damn if she didn't have one of the Colts strapped to her waist on a skinny little cartridge belt she must have had made to order somewhere to fit her. In fact all the outfit had been made to order. It fit her like you wouldn't believe and nobody could've took her for a man in daylight.

She put her mouth to my ear. "Saddles in there?"

"Yeah, two, three."

"We need 'em."

"There's men sleepin' all around."

"We must have them."

"They creak and all if you touch 'em."

"I know. But it's a long ride bareback, Timothy."

I had ridden bareback and I didn't like it. I went back inside. She stood with the gun drawn and in her hand. There was almost no light; it wasn't a pitch dark night but the sky was only partly moonlit, there were clouds. I never had such a job, keepin' the stirrups from clatterin' and huggin' those saddles to me like they were the love of my life. I'll never know how I got them outa there, but it had to do with Flo Quick and her ways, I can tell you that.

The buggy was all ready. She had hitched up the chestnut herself. We put the saddles into it and got in and led the horse to a safe distance away from the house. Then we got in. She drove to the south.

She said, "You better buckle on the gunbelt."

It was the first time I ever wore a gun and it was awkward. I managed to get it around me, asking her, "Did you see the Marshal?"

"That dolt," she answered. "He rode this way, you know."

"I thought he did from the sound of the horse." I wiped sweat from my forehead, although it was getting quite cool. "There is also a herder."

"Only one?"

"I believe so. Casey was pretty drunk."

"Ransom Payne and a herder. But we don't know what Payne will do. He's such a damn coward. Trouble with a man like him, you can't figure on him."

"He might ride through."

She said, "Casey scared him with the gun. We'll have to scout the herd. Can you be quiet in a field?"

"I was raised on a farm."

"You're a good boy, Timothy."

It was the quiet way she said it that got me. Nobody had ever bothered to give me much praise. Nobody had paid an awful lot of attention to me up until then. Knowing who she was and about the Daltons and all, it sure set me up. I began to feel like I could do anything that night.

I said, "If I can get a dab on a horse and saddle him up the rest will be easy. That is if these horses is broke."

"They're broken," she said. "They've been given the best of care. They're O-Bar-Z's best stock."

"Then how come they leave 'em out yonder with only one man? It don't make much sense."

"You'll find that people mainly don't make much real sense," she said. "If you think straight and consider the chances you can outsmart an awful lot of folks who think they are clever."

I had kind of noticed that myself, and also that the silent ones who seemed to be deep thinkers were sometimes just dummies who plain didn't have anything to say. I said, "The thing about horses is that they're scarey. And peculiar—they plain don't like some people. I get along good with them. It's too dark to tell which are the best of this bunch but if we can get aboard a couple we can cut 'em and pick 'em as good as possible."

"Any dozen or so will do." She was silent then, driving along the road. There were trees and bushes on each side and now there was a little more moonlight. Anyway, she had the sharpest eyes in the world and it was her that spotted a tethered horse. She drove past it, then pulled over.

"You want to try a scout? See if that's the Marshal?"

I said, "Sure." This was one galoot didn't scare me after I seen what Casey did to him. I took the Colt out of my holster and began sneakin' back onto the place where we had seen the horse. My boots was well worn and the ground thereabouts was soft, but I went slow and easy. I didn't learn this from no Indian—I learnt it from a mountany man returned to Missouri when I was a tad. He could sneak up on Nervous Nelly, the teacher who had eyes in the back of her head, and he used to do it, too, scarin' her to pieces and makin' us kids laugh. It was a matter of keepin' balance with your weight all distributed under you and feelin' every step before you shifted to go on. Though truly I didn't know what I was goin' to do with the pistol if he was awake and caught me spyin' on him, exceptin' show it to him like Casey did. I was doin' real fine, beginnin' to feel like a real mountain man when the screechy owl let loose from a tree limb, which luckily was not directly over my head. There was a wild yell and a gun went off.

"I see you in there, you devil. Come out and surrender. I am a law officer."

Well, that was Mr. Payne all right. I dropped down and lay still as a field mouse, which was probably what the screechy owl had tried to grab and couldn't. Marshal Payne thrashed around for a minute or two, then decided he'd been dreaming or something because he quieted down. I began to crawl backwards the way I had come and ran right into Flo Quick.

She said, "My God, I thought he had you."

"Not that damn fool. He didn't even get the owl."

We went back along the road together. She didn't have to come after a law officer, even one so pitiful as Payne, to rescue me. She didn't have to do nothin', it was all her own reckonin'. That was another thing about Flo Quick—if you was on her side, then she was on yours and there wasn't any dividin' line or nothin' that said she should stop and play safe.

I asked her, "What if he had shot me?"

"I'd have killed the sonofabitch," she said, and her voice was cold and tough.

I believed her. I didn't say any more about it but it sure made me feel queer that a lady like Flo would kill a man on account of me. I mean it made me feel I didn't know which of a way.

Soon enough we come to the south pasture. You could tell because there was a rail fence, not bobwire, and you could see a pair of the horses leanin' against the fence the way they do sometimes, a pair of them fast asleep. Then if you looked closer you could see some down in the field, some standin'.

The question was about the cowboy, the herder. Where was he? Flo drove all the way past the big pasture but we couldn't spot him in the night. So we got out of the buggy and unharnessed the Stapleton chestnut, which had carried us so far and so good, and turned him into the far end of the field, which made him very happy indeed—he rolled around and snorted and had himself a time. Then we pushed the buggy deep into a patch of trees where the brush was heavy.

Flo had to tote her brown satchel. Heaven only knows what was in it now. It never did seem big enough to hold all the stuff she pulled out of it from time to time. I made a blanket roll and tied it in the middle and strapped it across my shoulders. We took the two saddles and it was one hell of a load, but we didn't carry it very far, only to the edge of the O-Bar-Z pasture, where the good horses was.

Then it was scout some more. Only this time Flo decided to go along. We stashed the bedroll and saddles under the fence near a post so we could gather them up in a hurry and began prowlin' the field afoot, which seemed to me a dumb and slow and impossible job, what with sunup no more'n three, four hours away. But she said do it, and there was no way with her but to go along.

Like always, she had an instinct. The herder had bedded down and he was on the south end of the field, or nearest us. He figured if anyone stole a horse the way to go would be south, not toward the main house and all, and he was right. But he wasn't figurin' on me and Flo comin' on a scout to get him and then steal a herd of the animals. A proposition like that was away beyond his figurin', which was what Flo meant when she said most people were not very smart.

We come on him from both sides and used his own lasso to tie him up. He began to use bad language so we also gagged him with his kerchief, and blindfolded him too, because people that can't see get awful confused, so Flo said afterwards. Then I went in among the horses, who had been woke up by the cowboy's durn fool howlin', and it took a while to calm them down. But I managed to get aboard one and he only bucked a little. I rode him down to where we had left the gear and saddled him. Then I rode him back and turned him over to Flo. Then I cut out another one and did the same with him. Then I took down some rails and a thought come to me.

I said, "You know what? We can stampede this whole herd as well as a dozen of 'em. We get 'em started south and then Semple hasn't got his best horses to chase us."

"Now that's thinking, Timothy," she said. She looked like a boy on the horse, except in profile. She was laughing. "That is a real good notion. Let us proceed."

So we began rounding 'em up and chousin' them. It wasn't easy at night in a strange field. But we worked them awhile and got them goin' south. Then we picked up our bedrolls and began drivin' them all down the road. Some of them run off here and there but we didn't care. We could always handle ten or a dozen of 'em and after a while we begin to get the feel of the good ones, the ones with sand and bottom, and gradually we cut them out and left the others strewn along the way. It was a high adventure on an early morning, with the horses spattering along once we got 'em together like we wanted. Horses have got a herd instinct that works for you on a drive like this, and we didn't rush them nor yell at them; we talked soft and easy to keep 'em calm and just chivvied them along.

After a couple hours she said, "Can you handle them awhile?"

"I reckon. Why?"

"I'd like to drop back and see if they're after us when we get to the next rise."

The road was undulatin' up and down and we come to a rise which was pretty high for this flat country. Now it was coming dawn, and like always she had the right notion. But I thought I ought to stay back.

She said, "I can't handle them like you do. If anything happens head right for the South Canadian, you understand? Ask any Riley man the way—the horses will be your passport."

"I don't like it."

"I won't stay and fight if I see anything. I'll be right up with you in no time."

"Well, okay. But don't let 'em see you."

"I won't." We could see each other's faces now. There was a pink flush to the air. We were both high in spirits, but we hadn't had any sleep and we looked pretty tired. There were circles under her eyes and lines at the corners of her mouth.

I said, "We ought to stop and rest if they're not onto us."

"No. We can't take a chance."

"How long will it take?"

"We ought to make it by nightfall if we keep moving. There's grub in the bedroll, you know."

"Biscuits and cold meat three days old."

"There's a spring up ahead. We'll water the horses, rest them, eat and go on."

There was no arguing with her. She didn't come at you hard or anything, she just knew. But I couldn't help wondering when we would be able to stop if there was a posse behind us. And I didn't see how we could stand off Semple's rifles with our sixguns. I still had no notion of shootin' anybody for the sake of a dozen horses.

At the top of the hill she rode off the road toward a knoll, and this would give her a real long view. The horses were trotting easy, and now they had the notion they were to stay together. They had been in the pasture long enough to be willing to run; in fact, they hadn't been exercised enough and were carrying a little lard. This could be good or bad, dependin'. Good if we could mosey along and gradually work them down, bad if there was a hot chase with faster horses behind us.

It was a worrisome time. She didn't catch up and she didn't catch up. It was gettin' brighter all the time, a sunny day with some dark clouds ridin' a high wind. This was gettin' to be red claybank country with not so many trees, and I didn't like it. August could be hot as hell in this part of Oklahoma. I kept lookin' for Flo and strainin' my ears for the sound of shots I didn't want to hear. We went down a long slope of the road and then I heard her, and lookin' back I knew we were in for trouble.

She came up and I rounded the herd and stopped 'em and told her to get down. Light as she was, I wanted a fresh horse under her. I picked a likely looking roan and shifted the saddle, then decided on a big sorrel for myself.

She talked. "Just a cloud of dust but they're coming. Either we didn't tie up that herder good enough or that damn fool Ransom Payne roused 'em. We should've shot that bastard. Now they can catch us before we make the river—before we can make Riley's ranch. And anyway, Semple would love to take on Riley's people over stolen horses. We've got to get off the road."

I cinched up the second saddle on the sorrel. "They can track us easy any way we go."

"Not this way." She bit her lip, looking northward over the red clay. "It's risky. Fact is, Timothy, it's a real long shot. But it's either the hills or leave the horses."

44

"Leavin' them, that's a good notion."

"They're needed," she said. "They're prime heads."

"I figure our heads are prime, too."

She was nervous for the first time since I met her. Maybe she was a bit scared, but she didn't show that, only the lip-bitin' and the way her eyes canted around as though looking for an easy escape. "There's water, in fact there's a feeder stream. If it hasn't rained up there . . . There's no other way. I know the country. I don't know the whole layout but I think I know enough."

"You better know enough or our necks will be in a couple nooses. They'll string us up sure if they catch us."

"Not me." She tapped her revolver, hanging so heavy and strange-like on her hip. "I've got four for them and one for me. They'll never hang me."

"If we're goin' any place we better start," I said. No question about me, I was scared to death. Cuttin' out and leaving the horses seemed the only sensible idea to me.

"Down the road to where the bank slopes easy. I think around the next bend. I'll go ahead."

She was off without further palaver. I herded the horses along behind her, bunchin' them as best I could. The sorrel was a fine pony; he'd been cattle-trained and knew how to herd. We rounded the curve in the road and she was waving, all excited now, pleased as Punch that she'd been right. The claybank was solid enough because it hadn't rained lately and we put the horses to it. The whole band resented it but we got them up and onto a long, sloping stretch toward distant mountains. I knew we had to make those hills before the O-Bar-Z got within rifle range, and if possible, within sight of us. It seemed like too much for anyone without sleep to be able to make.

There was nothing for it but to gallop the herd. At first they seemed to enjoy it, but it was uphill and they wouldn't be any good to us windblown nor brokedown. We had to spell them. We began to sweat under the mounting sun. We kept looking back until our necks cricked to see if the posse was in sight. We couldn't talk. Our throats were dry and our bellies empty and all we could think about was the damn horses for the Daltons. It was plain damn dumb and I knew it all the time, but she had what it took to make us keep going. She had more of it than any man or woman I ever met in my whole damn life.

And that was the worst ride I ever had in my damn life.

First thing was the sun. You could look at it in the high sky of morning and know it would blister you all day. The clouds were all drifting northward. It was going to be a real bastard of a day under that sun.

Then when we hit the shale it was a slowdown because these horses were half of them unshod. We couldn't have them breakin' down their hooves. There was a mile or so of the loose rock, and this time I rode drag because she knew the way, or at least thought she did, and I sure didn't. I kept bendin' my back and starin' behind until the reflection of the sun on red claybank and various colored rock made me dizzy. Any minute I expected them to catch sight of us and come all out with rifle bullets flying.

She found a gorge. It was a sharp turn, then downhill. The going was smoother here. The saddle was cutting her butt and she was dripping with sweat, but she smiled like she was leading the cotillon at a town ball.

I said, "Take 'em down. I'll wait until I see 'em and then

we'll know."

"That's dangerous. I don't remember how far this canyon runs. We've got to find the water."

"You find the water. I'll find you. We got to know where we stand with this bunch behind us, how much we can rest the horses, how much time for waterin', lots of things."

She thought a minute and said, "You're right. I can handle them, there's no way for them to turn off. The way will be narrow for a few miles. Then if I do hit the water we'll drive in it and nobody could track us."

"They could guess we took to the water," I told her. "They must know the country, some of 'em."

"Yes. I'd better start."

She headed them down the gorge. She was tiny enough, and as she went away from me she seemed no bigger'n a minute and it just didn't seem possible that she could do what she was provin' before my very eyes. If she was good in bed, by gum, she was as good at everything else, and there never was nobody better at anything that I knew. Sittin' there in the hot sun and scared and worried and everything, I still wished there was time to take her down off that horse and lay her on some honest earth and do it to her once more. That's the effect she had on me, and many more than me.

I managed to get the horse into a piece of shade cast by a tall rock that stuck up like a sore thumb, but for myself I had to clamber that rock and squinch down and become part of it so I would not be skylined when the posse tracked us in. It was scarey and nervish-makin', but the longer it was the better for us because that would mean they was that much further behind us. I had a snack of stale bread and cold meat that was beginnin' to turn a little and made me kinda sickish, but a boy that age can eat most anything and survive. I knew I would need strength for that day. I was so sleepy I almost fell off a couple times, so I found a sharp rock and fixed me so that if I did nod I would lean on it and it would wake me.

It was a time for thinkin' too. A boy almost fifteen, in those days, who had been on his own for so long, had the tools for it, believe me. I knew I had been carried along by Flo Quick, but that seemed a good way to go. What was maybe bad was that Semple had seen me and Ransom Payne had seen me, and now that we had stole the horses my name would be mud . . . or at least my face would be known to them. I had crossed a bridge, and this part of the country couldn't hold me unless I was ridin' with the Daltons under their protection. I was on the way to being an outlaw, that's what it amounted to, and it was a very startling thing to face on that rock in that sun with men chasin' us with intent to kill.

Now you add to that the fact I had been cozenin' the lady who was Bob Dalton's girl, and that added problems about how I would act when I did meet up with the gang. I would have to walk mighty careful around her, I had already thought on that. There would be no pattin' her rump or feelin' those pretty boobies. There wouldn't even be any cantin' of the eye between us. I knew she would be all right, nobody could catch her out—it was myself I had to worry about. It was something to think real hard on.

And it put me to sleep. I must've missed the edge of sharp rock because I woke up with a start, sweating like a pig. I wiped my eyes and blinked and there they were, six or eight of 'em, away down as far as I could spy them, which was a good ways. They were dismounted, studyin' the track which led to the shale, and they were talkin' among themselves.

I slid down and held the nose of the sorrel and talked to it soft, although they couldn't possibly hear a snorting horse at that distance. I had to wait and see if they would come on or go back, or maybe—and this came to me and scared me some more—go straight for Jim Riley's ranch on the chance that we were headin' that way.

Well, they came on, but it was the way they did it that worried me. They came slow and steady. It could only mean they had decided they knew which way we had to go and were sure they had us. They could save their horses, and maybe they knew the country better than Flo, or thought they did. Either way they came like they knew exactly what they were doing.

I jumped into the saddle and headed the sorrel down the canyon. I rode hard and came out on the other side. I kept going up into the mountain trying to pick up sign, and for a while it was plain enough—which meant it would be the same for the posse. Then there was rock and hard ground and a turn south and a turn west. And here I lost the trail.

I took a chance and turned south, which was toward Riley's and where I believed from what Flo said there was the stream. In no time at all I knew I was wrong. There was no smell nor sound of water in that oven of a day in the hills.

There is one thing everyone knew, and that was not to panic when you was lost, and also to hit for high country. High gun, they called it. You kept above the enemy and he had to shoot upwards or climb to get at you.

I couldn't go back to the fork with the two ways because it would be a big risk. They might come slow but they might also have sent a scout out ahead in case of ambush. They might believe we were up there in the rocks with rifles to pick them off as they came. So I just kept climbing, and it got hotter and hotter. I had a sixgun, of course, and a box of bullets, but also I did NOT have the belly for a fight against eight men with long guns. It wasn't only the sun that made the sweat run down my back in a cold stream. I began to wonder if there wasn't a yellow streak just there under the rivulet of sweat.

Also it occurred to me about then that going up high was fine if you meant to stand and fight, but it also might give the people below a look at you. That was called bein' skylined and it was considered very dumb. Sometimes it seemed no matter what you did it wasn't too smart, and truthfully, no matter what anyone tells you or writes about, just about every tight like the one I was in did come down to a piece of luck.

There was no road up that hill. It was cuttin' here and there, ziggin' and zaggin' just to keep in motion, and tryin' to figure the next move. Then I come to a ledge, I swear the sorrel found it for us. From there I saw the stream.

It was away to the south and west of me. I saw the horses and the tiny figure of Flo, and she was stopped, lookin' back. I was afraid she would come back, like she did against Ransom Payne, but there was no way I could stop her. I stood up in the stirrups and waved my hat and motioned with both arms like a semaphore at the railway station. I don't know whether she seen me or not, but she did put the horses in motion and began following the

50

stream. Now I knew it was only a few hours from where she was to Riley's place, maybe nightfall. It was high noon by the sun—I had been asleep longer than I thought and I did feel the better for it, although still scared sweaty.

Then I looked back, and sure enough they had sent out a scout. It was Irish Casey and a couple of tough-lookin' riders. They were coming to the narrow gorge and I was almost directly over them on my ledge. Then I got an idea.

That canyon was awful narrow in one place. I got down off the sorrel and peered over the edge of my cliff. It was a good chance. I sat for just a minute. I could drop a horse, maybe get a couple men and block that passage for enough time to ride down and catch up to Flo. I was a good enough pistol shot for that. Only thing was I didn't have the sand to bushwhack anybody at all, no matter the danger to Flo, me, the Daltons, whatthehellsoever.

So I stared around with my mouth open. I saw a big round rock. I didn't have anything for a lever, though. But I did have a lariat that had been on one of the saddles I stole.

I dabbed the rope on the horn of the saddle. I made a loop around a tough shrub growin' out of the rock. I figured the angle and the chance, then I took the sorrel by the bridle and walked him until the rope was taut. Then I gee'd and hawed him a little. He was trained to the rope, he held it tight as a fiddle string.

Then I went over to the rock and waited. It sure was one big damn rock. I touched it and it didn't budge. I leaned against it just a little. I felt it vibrate, just a mite. Then I seen Casey right underneath me. There was nothin' to do but shove. I was scared the rope wouldn't fling loose and my horse would go down atop the Semple people. I ripped at the loop with my knife—every kid had his razor-sharp Barlow in those days and I was proud of mine. The rock seemed to grunt a little, or maybe that was me. Anyway it went topplin' over the edge of the cliff and sailin' like a bird down to the narrow place in the gorge. I coiled the rope and ran for the sorrel and was on the way without lookin' to see what happened. I heard a wild yell and a moan, so I knew it had been a true shot and someone had a busted bone or two and there would be a fine delay for the O-Bar-Z men.

I hit that water and both the sorrel and me had a time with it, good clear mountain water runnin' merry down toward the South Canadian proper, and then we were trotting along after Flo Quick and the dozen stolen head of horse. It was over an hour before I caught up with her.

She listened to what I had to tell and then she said, "Timothy, I wish we had time to stop right here so that I could give you a really good time on top of me for that. I truly do."

I said, "That would be dandy but I know I got to stop even thinkin' about it. I know I will get my tallywhacker shot plumb off if I don't stop thinkin' about you. Now we better get on and turn these nags over to the Daltons. Those folks back yonder are goin' to be kinda mad at us."

"They won't come onto Riley's place, not now," she said. "It'll be dark when they get there, and nobody goes prowling around Riley's after dark. It's very unhealthy."

We rode on, and like always she was right. And that's how I came to the hideout on the river, which Emmett Dalton had built so careful in a place where they could see in every direction necessary to keep the Marshals from catchin' them unexpected-like. Me and Flo Quick and a dozen fine head of horseflesh.

LIKE ANY KID, I GUESS I WAS EXPECTIN' to meet giants in the Dalton camp. Well, there's photographs of 'em all—everybody's seen them. They was to my eye even then a scrubby bunch. It's been said Bob was the handsome Dalton. With jug ears and little bitty close-together eyes, he didn't look even passably good to me. Emmett was younger and softer. They were the only two Daltons at the hideout at this time and it was sure disappointing to me, meetin' them.

Flo gave them the story of how we had stolen the horses, praisin' me to the skies. She told 'em I was eighteen although she knowed different by then, I was certain. All the time she was talkin' Bob had his arm around her and was feelin' up her boobies. It was a cinch he wasn't paying any attention to me, and neither were any of them exceptin' Emmett, who was only nineteen at the time and considered me his age and maybe someone he could brag to. He was a great talker always and the truth wasn't in him, then or ever.

It was him said, "Well, he could hold the horses for us when needed, Bob. If he's that good with 'em it might be a notion. They sure are a fine bunch he brought in."

"Him and Flo," Bob said. He was moony-calfin' at Flo all the time. "Why don't youall go and put 'em in the corral we built? They'll be good and safe in the brush."

Everybody sort of grinned, and it was easy to see the great Bob Dalton wanted nothin' but to be left alone with his gal and the bunks in the cave dug out of the riverbank. It was a huge cave and Emmett had done a good job of it, with little help from any of the others, you may be sure. They were a lazy bunch, too lazy to work at anything, even for their own comfort.

Big Creek Newcomb was a shrimpy little fella that always went around hummin' some dumb sing-song. Dick Broadwell had a thin nose and a faraway look and he showed a little breedin' but not much. He was just a castoff, a ne'er-do-well with a wild streak in him. Bill Doolin was a big man with a rovin' eye—he was probably the best of 'em, but he hadn't yet thrown off the notion the Daltons might pull off somethin' big that he could be in on. He often tried to take the lead away from Bob, and he would've been better at it, too, but the Dalton name was too much for him and he couldn't get others to side him. Bill Powers was medium sized and medium just about everything, not sayin' much, just followin' along, slavish to Bob. Way I seen it, they was a bunch of bums like I had seen around Coffeyville before the town got cleaned up. It didn't seem possible this was the famous Dalton Gang.

But there I was and it was safe for then and the O-Bar-Z people and Ransom Payne knew me and there was nothing to it but to stick around for a while and see what happened. Funny, I had got so ready for what would happen when Flo got back to Bob that it didn't fret me too much to go along with the others and drive the horses to the hideaway corral in the brush. I mean, I didn't like it but I had got used to the notion along the way, and there was already some things about Flo in her hard moments that I didn't care a whole hell of a lot for. I listened to the dirty talk of the outlaws without blinkin', knowing they were envious and wished they had their own girls up there on the South Canadian River in Jim Riley country.

They sure had filthy mouths, all but Emmett. It was a

funny thing, Bob and Emmett both worshiped the James Boys but only Emmett lived up to their moral way with women. Being only a kid himself, he didn't say anything at all nor try to stop them until Newcomb started on me.

"Hey, kid, what's your name—Younger? You come a long way with Flo—what about her?"

"She's a very fine lady," I told him.

"She's a good piece of ass, huh?"

"I wouldn't know."

"Shit. Flo likes her tail, everybody knows that. Sure, she saves the best for Bob, but she likes it any place he ain't."

"I wouldn't know if she was a man or a woman," I said.

Newcomb gave me a hyena laugh. "You're a goddam liar."

Well, in a spot like that it was good it was Newcomb. He was smaller than me anyway, although a growed man. I hit him right on the chin and he went spinnin' around like a top. I followed him and hit him again and he went into the bushes and lay there with his feet turned up.

Powers said, "Now you done it. When he gets up he'll shoot your dumb brains out."

I still had the revolver on me. I took it out, not being any fast draw nor any kind of a draw at all. "Let him shoot. No sonofabitch calls me a liar."

Powers said, "He didn't mean nothin', it's just his way."

"I wasn't raised thataway," I said.

Doolin hauled Newcomb out of the brush. The little man shook his head a couple times, staggered up with his back to me. Then he made a cat's move for his gun.

Before anybody could do anything Emmett kicked Newcomb in the butt, grabbed his gun arm and twisted it.

Emmett was a strong boy and Newcomb went spinnin' some more.

Emmett was yellin', "You know the rules. No fightin' among ourselves."

"He ain't one of us," Newcomb was squawking, trying to get away from Emmett. "I'll cut him up and make plowlines outa his guts."

Doolin stepped in then and took the gun away from Newcomb. He said, "You been hittin' that corn again. Now you listen to Emmett and you leave this here boy alone."

"I'll get you too, you double-crossin' bastard."

Emmett turned Newcomb a-loose and Doolin hit him. Doolin could hit harder than me. Newcomb slammed against a tree and his head struck and he went asleep again, this time real deep. Everybody laughed. Emmett started through a narrow path in the brush and we just walked along with the horses. They were too weary now to do more than lag their way to the corral, which was built tight and deep and would be hard to find if you didn't know the way.

The men fell to examining the horses, pleased with the quality of the stock, then rubbed them down with dry grass. Two things that bunch did good—take care of the mounts and shoot. That was about all they did have, but they were willing to work at them.

Emmett said to me, "Nobody even offered you any grub. That Bob and his women. You come on with me."

Even he didn't dare to go back to the cave and interrupt the festivities, but he was a strange one. He seemed to be prepared for almost anything. He had a food cache not far from the corral in case anything went wrong and they got cut off and had to ride out. He started a little fire. He had

a pan and eggs and some bacon and beans and hard biscuits and blackstrap molasses and everything, and he
could put it all together like a real cook—and indeed he
was that, and a good one. He could make skunk taste
good, give him a chance.

And he talked. He told me everything that had ever happened to him and his brothers. He told me about Julia, his
girl. He told me that there was something in the wind,
some job Flo and Bob knew about, and Doolin and the
others—but specially Doolin—was mad because they
didn't yet know. He told how Flo and Bill Dalton were
always lookin' for a job to turn and were good at it and it
was about time, for they hadn't any money left and supplies was runnin' low. If I had been a Pinkerton workin'
undercover the Daltons would've been in big trouble
when he got through cookin' and talkin'.

Me, I just stuffed in the good-tastin' fodder. Like most
country boys, no matter how much we knocked around
there always was somethin' to eat, and I never had been
so hungry. Emmett talked along and the others drifted in.
It had been twilight when we arrived, and now it got dark
and we sat around the fire. The darkness seemed to cool
down the outlaws and they jawed like other men, lazy and
fillin' their stomachs. Pretty soon Newcomb wandered in
and sat down and Emmett gave him a plate of food and he
stowed it away, havin' some trouble with his swollen jaw
but not sayin' anything, not even givin' any of us a hard
look. You could smell the booze on him now and I guess
he figured he'd been drunk and out of order, maybe not
even rememberin' real clear what happened to him.

They just set around, and pretty soon Newcomb finished eatin' and began singin' his miserable ditty about Bitter Creek, that which had given him his monicker. Then Emmett had a song, and so on. Not feeling like one of them, but not an outsider neither, I just sat and listened and watched the smoke from the fire, the real thin smoke of a good fire as it wound around on a stray little breeze now and then, or went right up straight toward the sky.

Then there was Flo and Bob. They walked in quiet while someone was singin' "Buffalo Gals" right lively and all joinin' in the chorus. Well, that was the first time I chimed in. It was because it hit me like a brick. There she was after the long hard day and you could see she had been enjoyin' it in the big hidey cave, all right, there was that look in her eye like she had done something great. I had seen that look after a long bout between her and me. It was like there had been a fight and she had won, that's what it was like. It dug me, and to cover up I sang along: "Buffalo gals won't you come out tonight, come out tonight, come out tonight; Buffalo gals won't you come out tonight and dance by the silv'ry moon. . . ."

I seen right away the score between her and me. She treated me like she was my favorite aunty. She was all kindness. Like we really had not known each other. It came to me that Bitter Creek had been right, foul-mouth or not, and I had been a liar and had no right to hit him. It was a lesson. Lots of times you have to attack in order to defend, even when you're wrong. Even nations do it. It's one of the ways of this world.

After a while we all went back to the hideout and Emmett made me up a bunk—he was a regular old granny about takin' care of people and not a bad fellow at all in many ways—and I was so dogtired I fell asleep and didn't even know where Flo and Bob Dalton slept, which is the good thing about being so young.

The next day Flo was gone.

Everybody was surprised but only Bill Doolin said anything, but he was always restless under Dalton leadership. There was an air of excitement, as if something was going to happen pretty soon. Emmett probably knew, but for once he wasn't talking. Bob was in high good humor for that time.

People would have you believe that all the outlaws did was sit around and plan and then rob and run and hide and then come out of their holes and spend their loot on women and booze and gewgaws and fancy clothes. Most of this was true, but it wasn't all business any more than other folks spend all their hours on business. For the time between late August and the day in September that Flo returned there was a sort of holiday air in the hideout.

Once accepted, the gang treated me like one of them, a youngster to be tolerated and taught. Bob Dalton was the best shot—he gave me lessons with the revolver, fast draw and all. Emmett was better with the rifle, but I never did get to be a sharpshooter, I just did learn how to squeeze off easy and relax and all that. As to the horses, they couldn't teach me anything, which they soon learned, and that became my job—a wrangler to a bunch of badmen.

They were badmen, all right. They had all the ways of the wild ones, the long riders. Life didn't mean much to any of them exceptin' Emmett, who longed for his Julia and played housekeeper and still talked on and on. He hadn't ever killed a man, but every one of the others had done so one time or another. And they were all thieves.

They had their excuses, like the James Boys, who claimed they were put upon and all. Theirs was the big squeeze the railroads were putting on the farmers, draymen, and taxpayers and landholders along the right of way. They were gettin' even for the Border people. Only, if they needed supplies or anything, they would take a bundle in the night. They left money on the counter, sure . . . but they didn't stop to ask the price of what they took. And they would have booze come hell or high water, however they could get it. Even Bob drank too much.

But Bob was a peculiar case. Of them all, he was the most interesting. He was always riding into danger to find newspapers. The only part of 'em he ever read was the stories about the Daltons, mainly him. There were plenty of stories. Like the James Boys, the Daltons were being blamed for every holdup between California and Missouri. If they'd been correct the Daltons would've had to own airplanes, which were not yet invented. There wasn't a gang ever operated that wasn't blamed for anything and everything that happened in the crime business. But Bob purely loved those stories. He'd take his Barlow and cut them out and save them like they were love letters. He'd read 'em aloud to the others, over and over, finding new lines to emphasize every readin'. One time Bitter Creek Newcomb, who was Bob's shadow and slave, mistakenly burned a paper before Bob got his clipping cut out. Bob knocked hell out of him and then made him ride all the way to Guthrie for another copy.

Another thing about him, he had a lookin' glass he had stolen some place and it hung over his bunk and he was always makin' faces in it when he thought nobody was around. Like he was a handsome character that the gals all loved. Flo wasn't gone a week before he was over in one of the farmhouses with a fat little old dumb amateur whore he had discovered. For a bandit leader and a so-called dandy—he dressed right careful—he was a plain pig. At least that's what I thought and kept to myself.

Bill Doolin was a different breed of cat. He was a big, husky, good-humored man, full of fun in a kind of harmless way. I'd been there a couple weeks when he showed up whilst I was carin' for the horses. He sat on the top rail of the corral and talked a bit.

"You sure know your way around hosses. Where did you learn all that?"

"Around and about." I wasn't talkin' any about my past, no more than they did—except Emmett.

"Yeah. You got a natural knack. What you think about this camp?"

"Me, I'm just a kid. I don't think much."

"You don't, huh? Then I'm a choir-singin' sissyboy."

That notion was funny. It made me laugh. "Thing is, Bill, I aim to mind my own business."

"Which is smart. You took care of Newcomb pretty good. Kept you from bein' down at the bottom of the peckin' order."

"You did pretty good your own self."

"He's a puke. The way he hangs around Bob is enough to sicken a man. Now he's got a little old gal maybe fourteen, that Rosa. She's got the morals of an alleycat. He couldn't get nothin' better no way."

"I wouldn't know about that."

61

"That little twist, everybody's had her. She ain't all that bad but I wouldn't touch her after Newcomb. I think he's got the old rall."

"Never had it." I grinned at him. "And I hope I never get it again."

That was a lie but it made him laugh, and it was always better to have them laughin' with you. For that matter, I wasn't against havin' Doolin leanin' my way. He was more man than any of 'em, even Bob. Only thing was, he hadn't yet got confidence in himself.

"Don't you get horny hangin' around here?" he asked.

"Man hasn't got any money, what good does it do?"

He said, "That Bob, he's chinchy, believe me. Everybody else is broke, he's got somethin' stashed away. He could spare a dollar for a whore once in a while. Men out here without women, it ain't healthy."

"I went broke bringin' in Flo and the horses."

"And Bob ain't even thanked you for it. Sometimes he purely gets my dauber down. Him and his newspapers and his lookin' glass."

"Well, he's the leader."

"And when Grat comes out of hidin' it'll be all Daltons. They stick together like pine pitch."

"Hang together or hang separate, someone said."

"Yeah. Well, kid, next time I get the urge I'm gonna take you with me. I got a place—it ain't in a town or nothin', matter of fact it's a pig farm run by a woman keeps a few girls around."

"That's real fine of you," I said. Make no mistake about Bill Doolin, you didn't cross him—specially when he wanted to do you a favor. He was a dangerous man. The

Daltons kind of had him mesmerized at this time, but he could have taken on Bob with fists or knives or guns and stood a better than even chance. None of the others was up to him in any way. And he had this smiley, good-natured way about him. Which was maybe why he didn't make an open break with the Daltons at that time. He liked people and he was easy-goin'.

Bob took advantage of Doolin that way. But it didn't always work. Like about the pig farm—Bob heard the woman had moonshine for sale and he felt too lazy to ride. So he lounged on the bunk and talked about it.

"Bill, how you feel about a gallon of that shine?"

"Oh, I dunno. I ain't all that thirsty and you know I'm low in the pocketbook." Doolin winked at me.

"Well, I got five dollars. Reckon that'd get us a couple gallon, wouldn't it?"

"Nope."

"It wouldn't? How come?"

"The revenuers been out. Shine is goin' for five dollars per gallon."

"That's highway robbery," said Bob.

"There's a lot of dishonest people around," said Doolin without crackin' a smile.

"Well, you mind ridin' over and pickin' up a gallon? We could all do with a little drink."

"I ain't got the fiver."

"Here, I'll loan it to you."

"I ain't borrowin'."

"Okay." Bob frowned. He hated being out-thought but he was a real booze-head and he wanted the drink. "I'll pay."

So we got the five and of course the shine only cost two

63

and a half and that left us enough for two of the whores and a half dollar profit. Doolin took me along for company, he told Bob, and that was that.

We came to the place and Doolin said, "Pig farm with pigs in the pen and pigs in the beds. Don't expect no dollies."

I was nervous enough with him sayin' that. I had never been in no whorehouse before in my life. It was a dark place, a long low building. There was a couple horses already tied to a rail and Doolin went to scout, making sure there wasn't any Marshals or other busybodies on the premises. In a minute he called to me and I went in the back door to the kitchen. Everything sort of revolved about the kitchen in those days, it seemed, although it was a funny place to pick out your whore. The woman's name was Bella and she was as fat as a butterball, but she was goodhumored and she liked Doolin. He gave her the four dollars and a half and the gals came in. There were only three of them, two being busy with the cowpokes.

One was tall and lanky and had a pimple on her nose, which was too long to begin with. Another had a couple of teeth missing up front. The third was fat and it turned out she was the daughter of Bella and had the same good-natured way.

It seemed Doolin liked fat ones and he knew the daughter, so it was up to me to pick between the pimple and the teeth that wasn't there. So I took the smaller one, she didn't look too bad if she kept her mouth closed. We went down along the outside of the building and she opened a door. There was a little lamp with a red shade and a bunk bed. There was a table with a pitcher of water and a basin next to the lamp.

The girl said, "All right, take it out." She lisped real bad on account of her teeth, but she was all business.

"Take it out?"

"I ain't doin' nothin' with anybody with a dose," she said. She had a cloth, which she dipped into the water.

"It's as clean as you are," I told her. I took it out and she examined it like it was a piece of steak she was buyin' in the butcher shop. Then she skinned it back and washed it. I didn't like it at all.

She had on a Mother Hubbard kinda thing. She took it off over her head and dropped onto the bed. "Okay, come on."

The sheet was a dirty grey. She wasn't a body, she was a hunk of flesh. She didn't even look at me, she stared at the ceiling. I felt dumb as an ox. My poor little thing just hung there. I didn't know what to do.

She said, "Most of 'em at least take off their pants."

That's what I needed—directions. I dropped my pants and went to the bed. She reached out and took hold of it and then it was all right. That is, it was workable—I wouldn't say it was really all right. The only difference between it and playin' with myself was that there was someone to talk to.

She had a little tired whore's patter about how good it was and all. I don't know who taught it to her, but with the lisp and the way she laid there like a hunk of beef it wasn't what you could call inspirin'. It was over before you could say Jack Robinson.

I said, "Thank you, ma'am," and put on my pants and went outside into the clean air while she washed herself. Like I say, it was the first time I had ever been in a whorehouse and it turned out to be the last. There just ain't any fun in one of them places. It's all made up and phoney.

We rode back with the jug and Bob Dalton gave everybody a drink or two and then got himself so soused he was snorin' half the next morning. Flo got in about noon.

She was ridin' a big black stallion, a beauty without a brand—not a ranch horse—with a curvin' neck and a high, fancy step. I held the bridle while she got down and run to Bob and into the cave. It was easier for me this time. I took care of the horse.

It was night when we all got together around a fire outdoors. It was September now, still warm weather. Emmett had made one of his fancy dinners and all he was concerned about was if Flo and the rest liked it. The others sensed something was up, however, and were pretty quiet until me and Emmett had cleaned things up and everybody was settin' around.

Bob did the talkin' but you could tell who had done the plannin', and it wasn't him. She sat atop a saddle under a tree and watched everybody's expression.

Bob said, "There's a town called Leliaetta over east. Anybody know it?"

"Near Wagoner," said Doolin. "It's a whistle stop."

"Just right. Well, Flo's been in Wagoner. She knows the telegrapher there."

She also knew Morse code as well as any railroader. Bob never bothered to mention details the like of that. He really did have the big head.

"That's the Katy," said Broadwell. "Not many settlers in that country yet."

"And there'll be a trainload of cash comin' through in four, five days," Bob said. "Cotton crop's been good and the money'll be goin' down to the banks in Texas. It's a cinch, and boys it'll be a big one. The biggest ever."

"Biggest we got so far is a couple thousand," said Doolin. "How we going to hit this choochoo?"

"Like before, only there's more of us," Bob said. "We all know how. It's what we get that counts."

Emmett said, "That's right. Enough to quit, maybe."

"Quit?" Bitter Creek giggled. "What in hell should we quit for? Anybody know a better way to make a livin'?"

Flo said, "Yes. Ranching down in Mexico. I've got some bad news, boys. The law is closing in on this place. They know Riley's protecting us. And Riley's men have been rustling cattle again. Semple at O-Bar-Z is telling it that we brought his horses in here."

"You mean we got to give up this place?" Emmett was heartbroken. He purely loved the hideout he had built on the bank of the river. He had a pair of old army field glasses he would look through for hours. He knew every squirrel, fox, deer, rider, anything that moved near us and a lot of things that didn't.

"After you hit the MK&T you can't come back," she said. "It'll give them the excuse and the nerve to move."

"After all my work," Emmett said. "I sure hope we do get enough to go south. I'll get Julia and never come back to this benighted country."

"Just how much you reckon might be on that train?" asked Doolin.

Before Flo could answer Bob told him, "It could be twenty, thirty thousand. It could be like Jesse done more'n once. I'll see the day when we top Jesse."

Flo was looking at me, and I thought she was sad. The others began jabbering about the big haul and what they would do with their share and she just continued to look sort of down in the mouth.

Finally she said, "The only thing to do is get out of the country. It's filling up and there won't be any place where the law won't be watching. Madsen and Thomas and Tilghman are picking up people every week. The Fort Smith court calendar is chock-full."

"They'll never get the Daltons," said Bob. "First place, we're smarter. Second place, we got too many friends."

"Your friends are weakening," she said. "The law can come down hard on poor folk. Rich folk want us all arrested."

"They got no chance with us," said he. "After the job is done we split up. Let the fuss die down. Then we'll meet wherever. Maybe in Mexico."

She said, "Yes, you've got to scatter. This should be a big one. I'm ready to go over the border."

"Sure, honey," Bob said. It was never possible to tell if or not he meant what he said. "We'll build us a real big ranch down there. We'll raise cattle and kids." He laughed loud.

I was out tendin' the horses for the night when she come to the corral. She waited 'til I was sure they all were ready for a long ride in the morning, and then we walked under the trees. Her voice was different, low and not sure.

"He's drinking again."

"You ain't surprised?" But he had not been drinking when she was there before.

"He won't quit."

"If we make a big haul he might quit."

"What do you really think of him, Timothy?"

"You want the truth?"

"Yes. I want to know. You're awful smart for a young

fellow. I'd like to know what you think."

"Doolin's a better man."

"I know that, but Bill's not a leader."

"Bob thinks too much on himself. Emmett is just a kid. What about Grat, where is he?"

"God knows. And Grat's worst of all, so don't count on him. He's an animal, and he drinks more than Bob does."

"Well, Flo, I think they're a sorry crew."

"A sorry crew." She bent her head as we walked slow in the forest. "Maybe you're right. The thing is, they're the only crew around."

"Why don't we pull out? That black and the sorrel I rode, they'd take us so far west nobody could find us."

"Timothy, I'm old enough to be your—well, your aunt. And I'm not like other women. I want things. I want big things. Oh, I'd love to settle down and have children. But not in any cabin. I won't be like these poor damn country women you see, all worn out and pitiful. I won't!"

"Well, there's big cities in the west, I heard tell. Denver, San Francisco. Plenty ways to make money."

She said, "There's only three ways for a woman to make big money, Timothy. Marry it, open a whorehouse, or steal it."

"If you had the cash you could open a store or somethin', couldn't you? Like in one of the cities?"

"And the way to get the money is through Bob Dalton. I'm into it and I'm stuck with it."

"He's awful stingy."

"Not with me. If I can get him away from the gang I can handle him."

"Not when he's drunk."

"I can make him stop drinking so much." She was firm and positive about it, and there was no use arguin'. And maybe she was right—she had her ways, that was for sure.

I said, "Truth to tell, Flo, I expected to see men like giants up here. What I see is Bitter Creek Newcomb, who I can beat at anything, and Bob readin' his news stories and Emmett cookin' and fussin' like a girl and the others, exceptin' Bill Doolin, just nothings. Sometimes they get to augurin' and they seem to me to be plain silly."

"They're different in a fight. Or a holdup," she said. "They've got the nerve when it comes down to it."

"What good's nerve without brains?"

She lifted her head and squared her shoulders. "I'm the brain, Timothy. Depend on it, I'm the brain."

She didn't sleep with Bob that night—he was drunk too early. The next morning we started at dawn for eastern Oklahoma, four, five days away. She didn't ride with us. She took the horses we didn't need and drove them into the Territory for sale.

Now here you had seven of us riding across country and a hundred law officers looking for us and the Daltons as well known as the President of the United States, maybe better in Oklahoma, and on stolen horses at that. It went to show two things: The Daltons did have people who protected them, either through fear or sympathy, and they did have nerve.

As we rode they seemed to change. They even looked different when they didn't shave, ate less, drank less, rode harder, lost weight. My own beard was beginning to get darker as I neared the age of fifteen, and one morning I looked at myself in a pool where I was gettin' a needed drink of water and almost scared myself to pieces. The face starin' back at me was like a wolf—or a coyote.

And tempers grew short, ridin' all day, sleepin' outdoors or in a friendly barn, washin' shirts without soap, all the discomforts. Bill Doolin and Bob Dalton bickered all the time. The others mixed in, Bitter Creek always with Bob and Emmett and me not countin', as I would drop back and stay out of it all. One thing about Bob Dalton, he had his instructions from Flo and he stuck with them, so everybody knew the plan and what each should do when the time came. I don't know how many times I was told where and when and how to hold what horses and keep them quiet if there was shootin' and have them ready to go when needed. I was told so often I got sick of it, but with them growin' nastier every hour I kept this to my own self. I had the old revolver on me, but I wasn't about to use it. I think if Doolin had started somethin' I might have sided him—but maybe on the other hand I would just have run away and left them to fight it out among themselves. You might say that by the time we got to that little burg with the peculiar name of Leliaetta, which must have been named after two or three gals strung together, I was somewhat sick and tired of the Dalton Gang.

I was also hungry, thirsty and tired. And somewhat scared once more. And we were all dirty and somewhat itchy. I hadn't yet noted the wild, free life of the long rider, the thrill and excitement of it.

It was September 15th when we rode into this little town, which was nothin' at all, just a country store and a crossroad. The MK&T tracks run past it, not through it. We laid up to get some sleep that afternoon, and at night we rode in toward the depot.

The store was closed. There was nothing to hear but barkin' dogs, which were every place you went. We could see the semaphore, and Bob checked his watch and we spread out. The train was due in a short time. The agent was also the telegrapher and he was readin' a magazine in his little office. This was a whistle stop. The engineer would slow down to see if a passenger or freight shipment was to be picked up, then he would yank the throttle and get speed again unless he had to stop. The idea was to get him before he could catch on to us and run away.

Bitter Creek and Emmett took up places on the far side of the track. Broadwell and Powers took the other. Bob and Bill Doolin had the tetchy job of stopping the train. I stayed loose with four horses and my own, the sorrel I had ridden to the South Canadian with Flo Quick.

Flo had taught me the signal of the engineer—four quick blasts to ask if he should stop. The semaphore would then bob an answer, in this case that the track was clear and it was okay to move along. That's when Doolin and Bob Dalton, mounted, would go into their act. It was a funny feeling settin' there on the sorrel wondering if it would time out. Over and over again they had planned it, but any little thing could upset the scheming. Flo had warned me of this. It depended on Bob and Doolin—the others were afoot for the moment and couldn't help a bit. Me, I was just a witness.

Many's the time I had listened for a train whistle at Coffeyville, wishin' I was on the train and goin' some place in the night. It was always a friendly sound, invitin' you to a party some fine place along the line. Now it was different—it was a danger, a lead-in to robbery and maybe killin', and for sure a lot of gunfire.

You could hear it comin' a long way off. I shifted in the saddle, got down and went to the head of the sorrel, holding the reins of the other horses, talkin' to them but watchin' up the tracks where the train had to come. First you saw the reflection of the giant headlight, movin' like a ghost and slowin' down as it came to the place where the whistle sounded. One, two, three, four just like Flo had said. All eyes were on the semaphore. If that telegrapher had spotted us he could warn the engineer, and furthermore he could send out a message that would bring a posse on us before we could ride out of the country. Broadwell had worked himself Injun fashion to the depot, keeping down out of sight but with his rifle ready.

There was a little minute, then the semaphore went into its dance.

Now the train was slidin' in slow and nice and the engineer was ready to give it the throttle as it came past the depot. Broadwell jumped in on the agent and drove him away from the key and out the door with his hands held high. I cut my eye to where Bob and Bill were ridin'.

They came in along the side of the tracks as the others let loose with a barrage of shots into the air. They could really ride and they were whippin' close to the engine. Everybody was rippin' out the rebel yell. Broadwell scared the station agent to death firin' off the rifle in his ear and whoopin' it up. Bob made the jump from his horse to the engine cab like a circus acrobat. Doolin fired in the air as Bob stuck a sixshooter in the engineer's ear and the brakes began screamin' and addin' to the noise and the train came to a stop.

Now passengers began pilin' out and somebody yelled

"The Daltons are robbin' the train," although they couldn't have known in the dark who in hell it was. The horses began stompin' and snortin' at all that clatter and I had to calm them down.

When I looked again the fireman and engineer were on the ground with their hands up and Bill Doolin was yellin' at the messenger in the express car to open up. The messenger was playing the hero and refusin', and Bill fired several shots through the door and told him that the next thing was dynamite to blow it open—and not do the messenger any damn good, neither.

Emmett held onto the engineer and fireman and Bob came down and joined Doolin in threatenin' the messenger. I thought that we didn't have any dynamite and if the messenger was really tough he would hold his own guns on the door and dare us to do anything about it. But they didn't pay those fellas enough to make 'em that brave and he finally opened the door. Bob jumped in and held out a meal sack—that was another thing he took from the James bunch, he always had some kind of sack for the loot—and the messenger said he couldn't open the safe.

Bob stuck his gun barrel halfway up the poor man's butt and cocked it. He said, "This won't feel real good if I pull the trigger."

So the safe was open. But now the passengers were millin' around on the ground and gettin' out of hand. The orders had been strict—don't shoot anybody unless we were fired upon. But a lot of the passengers were certainly armed—near everybody was in those days. Doolin got real upset about these people and fired his rife over their heads.

Bob said, "Don't do that. Just take this sack and lemme

down from here."

But Doolin loved breakin' Bob's rules and orders. He rode down on the passengers, firing in the air and cursing them something fierce. That did it. They broke like sheep. They piled back into the cars. We were not going to rob them—it took too long and the haul was never very big, and anyway the sack full of loot looked good. Bill Doolin took it from Bob and hung it on his saddle and waved and I came in with the horses. Everybody mounted up and we was out of there slick as silk, laughin' and hootin' and excited like kids on a picnic.

We rode west and we rode fast. Funny, not a soul of the few people in that town of Leliaetta even lit a lamp or otherwise provided a target in any way, shape or form. Maybe they didn't like the Katy, or maybe they liked their skins whole, and maybe they figured it was best not to be able to answer questions later when Ransom Payne and the Marshals came trailin' along.

And for the little while as we were ridin' away from that place there come the thrill of the hoot owl trail. The very nerve of takin' the money from the train was a boost, it felt good to be with the gang, all laughin' and celebratin.' We stayed together that night, puttin' lots of miles between us and the railroad. Everybody was wonderin' how much we had got and talkin' about what they were goin' to do with it and all, and Doolin got tired of totin' the big sack.

"This damn thing keeps bangin' my knee," he said. "Why don't somebody else take it awhile?"

That was Doolin, ever trustin' people. He was kind of a decent man thataway. Bob grabbed the sack and nobody heard him complainin' about how uncomfortable it was.

Not Bob Dalton. He didn't talk about Mexico none, either, like he had with Flo Quick. I was ridin' next to him most of the night and I noticed how he simmered down before the others. Emmett kept yapping about Julia Johnson and how he couldn't get to her fast enough, but Bob let it all go by. And pretty soon Doolin quieted down, and then I thought it was comin' before this hooraw was over—the open clash between them, Bob and Bill. It was in the air. I could actually smell the thing growin' bigger between them, and it was a cinch Doolin wished he hadn't of turned over the sack of loot.

When it was daylight we were safe enough for that time. We pulled up in a clearin' somewhere in the center of a scrubby forest. Everybody got down off their horses and rubbed their hands like a storekeeper itchin' for his money. Everybody looked at Bob Dalton.

He said, "This here is as good a place as any to split up."

"Yeah," said Doolin. "I'm all for goin' back to Arkansas myself. Maybe I'll start a little ranch and raise apples. Always did have a hankerin' for apples."

"Me for old Mexico," said Powers. "I'm with Bob and Emmett on that."

"Me too," said Bitter Creek, who was always with the Daltons.

Broadwell didn't say anything, and of course neither did I. Nobody had said anything about my share, and truth to tell I had that smell in my nostrils, which had been growin' all night on the ride since Bob got so quiet.

Now Bob held the sack and moved over so that Emmett, Bitter Creek and Powers were ranged beside him. Broadwell and me were over a ways, apart from them but not with

Doolin neither. Bob reached into the sack and began takin' out bills and coins. He stacked it on the ground and every-body hunkered down. He handed the sack to Emmett, who took it and walked to his horse. It wasn't plain daylight in the woods and nobody could be positive sure, but what with the way I'd been thinkin' and one and another other things, I could have swore that sack wasn't empty by a damn long shot when Emmett tied it to his saddle and stood by it. I know this wasn't Emmett's thinkin' but I also knew Emmett would follow Bob's orders down to the bricks, if any.

Bob was countin' the loot. He began to shake his head and look woeful. He said, "Why, this ain't near what we thought we had. This here is like Wharton that time. We been cheated again. That damn Flo, she had the wrong information."

"She did, huh?" Doolin was cold, and I thought he was ready. He slanched his eyes around at the rest of us. Nobody said a word. There was Emmett over by the sack and the horse with a rifle right at his hand. There was Bitter Creek, who didn't have a brain in his miserable head and believed everything Bob uttered was gospel. There was Powers, who also was not too bright and was a Dalton man. And there was me and Broadwell, who didn't have enough guts to speak up.

I don't know about Broadwell, who was a moody sort, but I do know I might have sided Doolin. It was sort of up to him. He was supposed to be a brave man and a coming leader of men. It's a funny thing about outlaws, you can't depend on which way they will jump. Right then and there Doolin could change the course of a whole hell of a lot of lives if he made his move.

Bob had the money all separated into little mounds. He made his voice real mournful. "This here is enough. Three hundred apiece? We can do better'n that turnin' square."

"Three thousand, did you say?" asked Doolin.

"I wish to God it was. You see it there, Bill. A pukin' three hundred."

Doolin looked over at Emmett. Then he stared at me and Broadwell. Since then I thought a million times, I thought how everybody is ruled by fear. Only a crazy person has no fear. The fear makes everybody figure the odds. It's real easy to be brave if you're insane or if the odds are with you or if your life is in danger or a loved one's life is in danger. But in a case like that, everybody sittin' around knowin' it could be a shootout which would kill maybe half of us, that cold fear grabs you by the throat.

Doolin said, "Three hundred. That's the divvy, huh?"

He was inchin' around, and it looked like he was going to draw and duck behind a tree and get to shootin'. I made ready to dive under some bushes and use my revolver just to save my skin.

Bob made his voice real mournful. "Well, this is the end."

"End of what?" Doolin was suspicious.

"End of the road for me and Emmett," said Bob. "This here shows it don't pay no more. Nothin' is like it was. There ain't any profit in robbin' trains."

Doolin said, "Maybe you'd like to try a mint?"

"I don't aim to try nothin'. The Daltons are through, boys. Finished. The gang is busted up."

"Busted?" Bitter Creek seemed about to cry. "No, Bob, you can't leave us like that."

Powers was frowning. "You're funnin', Bob."

"No fun. The whole thing ain't fun, comin' up with this little amount of money for all that work." He wrapped his end of the loot in his neckerchief.

Doolin said, "Turnin' yellow, huh, Bob?"

That was an insult, but Bob Dalton was never one to overplay a hand, not when he was sober. He look sadly at Doolin and said, "Let's part friends, Bill. I don't think anybody believes I'm yellow. No Daltons is yellow."

Bitter Creek said, "Sure, Bill. Everybody knows that."

It was no use and Doolin knew it. Bob had swung it—if it ever was in doubt—when he said the Daltons were quitting the business. It addled what little brains they all had. Doolin picked up his share. He hesitated just a minute— and was beat. He walked to his horse and said, "So long, gents. Spend your hard-earned cash in good health."

He took one more hard look at Emmett and the sack from the train and then at Bob. He mounted and rode out.

Bob said, "Well, boys, I've made up my mind. Me and my kid brother will just mosey along."

Bitter Creek and Powers acted like they were parting from blood brothers. Powers didn't say much, but he went with Newcomb as they rode off. Broadwell just shrugged his shoulders and told Bob that he'd be wherever if Bob changed his mind. I didn't know what to do. There hadn't been any cut for me.

Bob said, "Timothy, you ride with us."

"I don't know," said I. "Chris Madsen and the other lawmen'll be after youall. Seein's I don't get any part of even three hundred maybe I better take off west."

Bob said, "We're meetin' Flo. She said to be particular about you on account of you're so young and she takes a motherly interest in you. I hold with motherly feelin's. Us Daltons got the best mother in the world."

"That's the God's truth, bless her," said Emmett. He had been quiet for so long guardin' that sack that he was spillin' over. "We'll be seein' her on the way. We always see her to let her know the law ain't got her brave sons. Our dear, good little mother, she must never suffer for our outlawin', that's the creed of the Daltons."

I never heard anything more nonsensical in my life, but if Bill Doolin didn't cross 'em, who was I to get sarcastic? I figured I might as well ride along with 'em and maybe learn what was really in that sack, and anyway the one I had any confidence or faith in at all was Flo, and they were headin' her way, so hell, I rode along.

The place they was to meet her was near Guthrie, which was the Territorial Capital, and this had to be Flo's thinking because the Daltons would never have that much brains. The ranch was right under the nose of Madsen and Thomas and them, a place they would not think of looking. Emmett dropped off to go see Mother Dalton like he said he would. Bob kept the sack in his bedroll, and him and I rode on.

The ranch was a small place but real nice. There were a few horses, which Flo had got one way or another, and some chickens and a cow—just a little farm which she had made a down payment on from the money she got sellin' the horses we had stolen from O-Bar-Z and one thing and another. Flo could always come up with money—not a whole lot of money, but enough to get along.

We rode in at nightfall. Flo came out of the house in a frilly dress and Bob grabbed her and hugged her. I sat on the sorrel. Flo looked at me over his shoulder and in the dusk I could see she wasn't smiling like she was over-joyed nor nothin'. It gave me a queer feeling.

I took the horses around back. I didn't dare poke into Bob's bedroll, although I thought about it. I unsaddled and rubbed down and curried and combed and brushed and fed. I took my time, thinkin' that Bob might already have her in the bed for a quick one, knowin' how piggish he was, not bathed nor anything. But she called and I brought our bedrolls into the house, his and mine.

He was in the kitchen and he already had a bottle open. She put food on the table and I ate the first hot meal in a long time and it was mighty good—she could cook almost as good as Emmett. Bob drank and Flo had one with him, but only one.

She said, "The word is out. The telegraph had it that you got three thousand. That's the railroad's figure. The news-paper had it seventeen thousand."

"What's your guess, Flo?" Bob was chuckling, pouring whiskey—it was better than the usual moonshine.

"Somewheres in between."

"You believe somethin'?"

"Like what?"

"I still don't know how much." He roared with laughter. I swabbed my plate with a heel of bread. I believed him. He was a strange man. He had counted out part of the money and handed the sack to Emmett and he had got it back from Emmett, giving his own brother a few dollars out of his pocket to give their own mother they were always maun-derin' about. I had not seen him even look into that sack.

She said, "You gave the boys a bad count, then?"

"What else? Those dummies, they're hired hands far as

I'm concerned. They get hired-hand pay. Timothy, gimme that bedroll—never mind, just dig out the sack."

I went to where I had put the bedrolls in the corner and unrolled his. The sack was right in the middle, and of course it wasn't empty. I brought it to the table and Bob dumped it. Money fell all over the place—on the floor. No coins—he had divvied up the coins, which were mainly silver. It was a lot of money. We all helped pick it up. Bob was a little drunk already and laughin' fit to kill.

Flo smoothed it out and organized it in piles. When she was finished she said, "You should've given the boys their share."

"Like hell. Doolin like to try and shoot it outa us but he lost his nerve. Called me 'yella' he did, and I had to snicker, knowin' it was him and not me and knowin' he knew it."

She said, "Bob, there's seventeen thousand almost."

"Why, sure. I knew it was our biggest haul. Hell, Jesse took more'n that plenty times. We're just beginnin'."

I said, "I thought you was going to quit?"

"Boy, you got a lot to learn," he said, laughing again. It was his night to laugh a lot. "You want to cool 'em down, you give 'em something to think about. I knew old Bitter Creek would start to snivel. It distracted old Doolin, too—you seen it."

He was right. I looked at Flo and nodded. That was the way it had been.

She asked, "Well, what now? How much do you and I take?"

"Half."

"It's enough."

"Emmett gets the rest. He can split it with whoever—

Grat if he comes in, Bill, I don't care," said Bob. "Emmett was there, he gets half. That's the Dalton way."

It sure was. Cheat everybody else but split it with the family. Now he was staring at me.

I said, "I ain't sayin' anything. It's your business."

"The others got three hundred. You get six hundred. And you keep your mouth shut. You understand?"

"You know me to talk a lot?"

"You wouldn't be here if I figured you for a talker," he told me. "You're just a boy but you shut up good. Here, take the six hundred. It's a stake if you ride out."

Flo said, "Why should he ride out?"

"He don't have to. But maybe he didn't like it."

"None of my business," I told him again. "I'm the wrangler. Do I get to keep the sorrel?"

"You certainly do," said Flo. "And you've got something coming from the sale of the others we took from O-Bar-Z."

"Whatever you say," Bob agreed. He could rave and rant and play the big man, but Flo had his number. He depended on her when he was drunk, when he was broke. He was fair with her on the cut because he knew she was too smart for him. I don't think for a minute he loved her. He never loved anybody exceptin' Bob Dalton—and the memory of Jesse James. I heard him cuss Jesse and Frank and the Youngers, but the memory of them, the amounts they stole and the years they got away with it, that he loved, that was his cherished dream. Right now he was getting drunk pretty fast.

Flo said, "I fixed a place for you out in the barn, Timothy. It's a nice little sleeping place. Come, I'll show you."

"You sure treat him nice," Bob said, finishing another glass of the booze. "That's decent of you, Flo. He ain't a bad kid at that and he sure knows horses."

I said, "Well, good night, Bob," and followed her out to the barn, which was quite near to the house. A dog barked and she shushed him and we found a lantern and struck a lucifer made of wood, one of the new kind she had, and there was a ladder going up to a hayloft.

She said, "There's a good new bunk up there. I think I'm going to need you, Timothy. Will you stay by me?"

"I thought you were headin' for Mexico with all that money."

She shook her head. "You see him in there. You hear him. He'll never give it up. Tell me, how did the others take that story of his?"

"They believed him."

"Doolin?"

"It's hard to tell about Bill. He almost jumped Bob. Then he quit."

"Doolin's smart but not smart enough. None of them are smart enough."

I said, "You're smart enough."

"I wish to hell I was. I wish I was smart enough to get out. Now all I can do is study out another job. And spend some of Bob's money." She looked hard at me. "What are you going to do with your money?"

"Buy some clothes."

"Fancy duds?"

"Workin' clothes. And I'm hidin' the rest of it. I'll give it out I lost it gamblin' but I'm stashin' it away."

"If you were a few years older," she said. "Or me a few years younger . . . well, go on up and get your sleep, Timothy. I know you must need it. I'll go back and try and make some sense out of him before he gets too drunk."

She had fixed up a corner of the hayloft, hangin' a horse blanket to make a private room. There were hooks on the wall and a little bureau with wash basin and all, and the new bunk had clean blankets and a shuck mattress. It was pure luxury, specially after the long ride back and forth to Oklahoma. When she had a mind Flo was a homemaker.

I hid the money in a boot and kept my revolver handy. When a fella has nothin' he don't worry, he just goes along from day to day. But when he gets a little he starts protectin' it and thinkin' about it and how to get more. If the whole Dalton gang had tried to steal my six hundred dollars that night, some of 'em woulda roasted in hell before they got finished.

That's why I woke out of a sound sleep when there was a noise in the barn. I grabbed the gun and slipped off of the bunk and rolled under it. I cocked the Colt and waited. If it was Bob I was sure goin' to hold him 'til he explained why he didn't call out before he started climbin' that ladder.

The next thing I heard was a whisper, like a whimper. "Timothy? Timothy, are you awake?"

I dropped the gun and crawled out from under the bunk. There was a bit of moonlight comin' through the roof where it was cracked and slitted. Flo had on a night robe and slippers and that was all.

I said, "Holy Cripes, Flo."

She came to the bed and sat down. She said, "He was too drunk to do anything. Too drunk. He slapped me."

I said, "Maybe I ought to go down and finish him."

"Would you do that?"

I thought about it. "If I had to. He's got no right to hit

you. He's nothin' without you."

"The trouble is that he's nothing with me."

I said, "I don't see any sense in this. None of it."

"Don't look for any sense." She put out a hand. "Come and sit with me."

I said, "I better get my gun handy in case he wakes up."

"The devil couldn't wake him to take him to hell."

I sat beside her. It came to me that she had been without for some time. I knew the way she was. She had to have it. She had been waiting for Bob and there he come all drunked up, not givin' a damn about anything but himself, like always. She put her head against me and cried a little, and it was more than wantin' a man, although that was a big part of it also. She'd been schemin' and plannin' and wantin' to go straight down Mexico way and he had let her down. It was a whole hell of a lot wrong and she was discouraged. It was the first time I had seen her like that and it made me sorrowful. Sure, she was an outlaw and all that and had done things here and there, but she had been better to me than anyone I'd ever knowed. She was the only friend I had in the world.

So I put my arm around her. I didn't even think about not havin' anything on but my undershirt. She stopped cryin' in a minute and didn't say any more, just lay against me lookin' at the crack in the roof of the barn. The horses stirred below and a night bird called. I kissed her on the cheek and she turned around and there we were again.

It didn't make any difference that I was a substitute for her man who was only half a man. It didn't make any difference about anything. I was goin' on fifteen and I knew her and she knew me and we knew what to do to make the world stop for several hours. And the hell with Bob Dalton or anyone else. It was just the two of us alone against the whole goddam life we had to lead.

They sure needed me. Neither of them were worth a hoot around even a small farm like this one. They could help take care of the horses, but Bob was drunk most of the time and Flo kept making trips here and there to get information. I milked the cow and fed the chickens and gathered the eggs, and when Flo was away I did the cookin', about which everybody complained. I say "everybody" because it wasn't any time before Bitter Creek showed up, then Bill Powers, then Dick Broadwell. They would come and go, and what they did for a livin' besides borrow off Bob when he was drunk I never did know. Flo hated having them around and often took off whilst they were there. She was gone and Bob was just starting to yell for his dinner one noontime when two riders came to the house.

I never heard such yellin' and hollering outside of a train robbery or a county barn dance. I came out of the kitchen not knowin' whether to shoot or wait for orders. The three of them were rasslin' around in the yard like kids in a schoolyard is the way it turned out. Then one big jasper got Bob and the other one down and laughed like a coot and I knew who it was. There was no mistakin' those narrow-set eyes and jug ears. It was Grat Dalton.

The other one favored Emmett. He wore spinach whiskers and no mustache, and that had to be Bill. The missin' links had arrived, the other pair of badman Daltons.

Grat was the oldest, born in 18 and 61, but his brain didn't grow much along with him and he always seemed the youngest. Bill was two years behind him and looked older. Bob, who was only twenty-one at the time, was the leader and most mature—Emmett seemed much more'n two years behind Bob. They were an odd bunch no matter how you figured them.

Bob saw me with the gun in my hand and bawled out, "Timothy, this here is family. Put down that hawgleg."

Grat got up. He was a big one. He was gaunted at that time but you could see the power in his shoulders. He grinned like a hungry wolf.

"Emmett said you had a cub around. You got some grub ready, young un? I'm purely starvin'."

Bill said, "Howdy, young feller. Emmett's down the road apiece, we beat him in. He's bringin' some beef."

"How come he's behind yawl?" asked Bob. "You shouldn't oughta leave the kid alone, the way the Marshals been crowdin' us."

"Somebody stole his good horse." Bill laughed like it was a huge joke, which in a way it was, of course. "He hadda grab a crowbait out of a farmer's back lot."

"Stole his horse? Where was Emmett?"

"Sparkin' his Julia," Bill said. "He gets real careless when he's around Julia."

About that time Emmett came in view. The horse he was ridin' was a plough animal, not worth a dollar and a half. I'd never seen him so mad. He had a hindquarter slung beside his saddle and he was spurrin' the poor beast and cussin' and bellowin' and sweatin'. I was glad to see him—I didn't need all the damn Daltons bitchin' about my cooking.

Emmett yelled, "Timothy, come take care of this damn four-legged hunk of dogmeat."

I went to help him unload the beef and his bedroll. We took off the saddle and tried to shoo the horse away. He wouldn't leave. Emmett was all for shootin' him but I got him away and into the stable and fed him some hay. Poor old thing, he was plain confused.

Grat was yelpin' that he couldn't wait for any barbecue, he wanted food and plenty of it right now. He had an ignorant way of speakin', worse'n any of the gang. He came down on me right away.

"I hear you're a wrangler, boy. Wrangle me up some vittles, you heah?"

We were in the kitchen and there was a pot of coffee and some beans on the stove. There was a loaf of bread on the table. I looked around and then turned my back on him.

"You see it, you can help yourself."

He made a grab for me. He was big and mean, as mean a man as ever walked. He'd been in jail and on the cross-country trek and he was sore as a bear. I was almost as big as him but only a kid, so I didn't try to duck. I just stared at him. He pinched hard onto my shoulder.

Emmett came in the back door. He said, "Leave him alone, Grat. He's all right."

"Like the damn hell he is, back-talkin' me. I'll larn him who's boss around here."

Emmett picked up an iron skillet and said, "Bob's boss around here. Timothy's proved himself."

"You gonna hit me with that skillet? Why boy, I can whup you, the iron pan, and this one together and think nothin' on it."

"Why don't you try that?" I asked him. "Turn me a-loose and try it."

He let go of me, which was a mistake, since I had learned how to get along with these people. I kicked him in the shins.

He howled, jumping on one foot. I was going to wallop him alongside the ear but Bob and Bill came into the kitchen and got in my way.

Emmett said, "Grat's up to his old tricks, pickin' on Timothy. He'll never grow up."

"You damn punk kid," Grat yelled. "You're as bad as him."

Bob said, "Shut up, Grat. Put down that skillet, Emmett. You, Timothy, cool down."

He was, remember, twenty-one years old at this time. Bill was twenty-eight and Grat was thirty and a big, ugly, hulkin' brute. But we all calmed down. When it came to the pinch it was easy to see who was really the boss.

Grat said, whiney-like, "I'm hongry."

"Then eat. We got things to talk about. Flo will be here any time, now."

Bill said, "That's right. I seen Flo and she's got information for you."

Grat stomped to the stove and began gobbling cold beans and chawing on bread, grunting like a rootin' hog. He had no concentration—a thing done was a thing forgotten and it wasn't easy for him to start any train of thinkin'. He was all animal. He spoke with his mouth full.

"Bob and his hoors. Just show me a train t' rob. I got to get even. Them California railroad people put me in the can and I need to get hunk."

"You'll get your train," Bob said.

I was about to say something about Grat using a dirty

word on Flo, but if Bob didn't take it up it figured better for me to keep my mouth shut. As long as I was with the gang it was best not to get too many of them mad at me, and I already had Bitter Creek against me. And after all, when I stopped and thought, Flo wasn't exactly any nun.

I went outdoors. It was always better out there. The cow, the chickens, the horses were clean, they were what they had been born. I was there when Flo rode in, and talked to her before she went into the house.

"Honey, I'm dead beat," she said. She looked it. She was twenty-two or three but she moved as though she was middle aged, dismounting, walking into the stable with me. "That damn fool Ransom Payne is on our trail. Of all the lawmen, he had to get some information from some damn squealer."

I said, "Grat's here."

"I know. Bill told me he was coming in, the dumb beast."

"He wants a train."

"I'll buy him a toy one on tracks."

"Bill thought you had somethin' set up."

"I did. It's fouled up. Madsen and Thomas and Payne. Two good men and a fool. Get ready to leave, Timothy."

"Where to?"

"Oh, I've got a place. Old Flo. She always has somewhere to hide out. Greer County in Texas for now. Until things blow over."

"I don't think Bob's got much money left."

"Of course he hasn't. He spills more booze than most people can afford to drink. And there's Emmett and Bill, and now it's that goddam Grat."

I said, "Flo, here we go again. Let 'em go to Texas. We

can get away. The sorrel and a little bay out yonder will take us wherever we want to go."

"This is the second time you made that suggestion. I reckon I'm crazy not to take it. But the Red Rock plan is so good—maybe we can pull it off later. One big strike and next time I take my share and run. If Bob won't go, then the hell with him."

"Sooner or later we'll all be in Judge Parker's court."

"No. That's where Bill is valuable. He may not be the world's greatest politician but he's making some money in land and he spends it in the right places. And he trusts my word. No, we just have to lay low for a while."

I said, "Too bad it can't be here. This is a nice place, Flo. I could farm this place right good."

"I wish you could stay. But Payne knows you and Semple knows you."

"Yeah. I go where you go. It has to be that way."

She put her hand on my cheek. "Yes, Timothy. It has to be that way."

She went into the house. I took care of her horse. Then I shoved my gun inside my belt and pulled my shirt over it and entered the house through the kitchen door. They were in the next room and I listened. If anything went wrong I figured to take Flo out of there one way or another. When you live with outlaws long enough you get over bein' scared by them. If you don't look out, you'll get to be just like the bastards.

Grat was hollering in that big boob way of his. "Ransom Payne is a piss-ant. That bastard couldn't catch a chicken in a hen yard. I say we lay for him and finish him and go on ahead at Red Rock."

"You don't know Chris Madsen," Bill said. "That Scandahoovian is one smart apple."

"Then kill him, too. What's the matter, we gettin' soft or somethin'? I been a long time without."

Bob said, "Now, Grat. Everything we got is yours, big brother. We can do what Flo says."

"The hell with your goddam woman."

Bill said in his smooth way, "I happen to know her word is good. If she says they're on their way here you can take it for gospel."

"I couldn't give a shit where they are. I'll fight 'em alone if I gotta. You, Flo," Grat yelled. "Who you been screwin', you know so much? Anything I hate is a smart hoor."

Flo said, "Does it matter how I found out? If we don't clear out of here today they'll be on us with a posse. And the rewards are dead or alive."

"Why, you goddam. . . ."

Bill interrupted him. "Grat, you haven't even seen Mama yet. Now you know that ain't right. We can all take off and visit with her in niggertown, and then we can go our ways."

"What ways?" But he was calmed down, so I took my hand off my revolver butt. "Where do we go?"

"I've got a place in Texas," Flo said. "Soon as I was sure I got hold of a . . . friend . . . and we can have this safe place in Greer County."

"I purely hate Texas."

"Texas horses can be stole as good as any," Bob said. "We got a stake. Flo knows how to get more."

"Fuckin' people," said Grat. "I know how she gets it."

"None of your business, is it?" Bob was calm. "Brother Bill agrees with her. I go along. Emmett goes along."

Emmett spoke for the first time. "I better see to the beef—we can take it with us. Yes, I got to agree with Bob."

He came out to the kitchen and I knew it was over and Flo and Bob had won. I started out the back door but I wasn't fast enough and Emmett spotted the gun. He followed me into the yard and took my arm.

"Timothy, don't you never tote a gun against the Daltons. We squabble among ourselves, sure. But don't you ever interfere or you'll be killed. You hear that?"

I said, "Grat might've started a ruckus."

"Not against us brothers. He'll beller a lot but he never will. You got to know by now, the Daltons stick together. It's like a religion or somethin'."

I said, "All right, Emmett"

"You just remember. And maybe you better not go to Texas with us, neither."

"That's all right with me."

"Bitter Creek will be around. Grat already don't cotton much to you. Maybe you better stick with Flo if she can cover you against the Marshals."

"Well, I dunno." Of course that was what I wanted more than anything, but I couldn't let on.

"You got some money. Flo's damn good at coverin' up. I'll talk to Bob about it."

"Anything you say, Emmett. You been good to me."

He let go of my arm. "Well, we're the youngest. And you always mind your manners, leastways around me or unless someone tries you out. But you remember what I say. The Daltons stick together, first, last and all the time."

He was right. And I didn't go to Texas, nor did I see the Daltons again until the followin' May of 18 and 92. I spent that winter with Flo off and on, and what she did to get money for that crowd was catch on with an old butcher named Mundy in Guthrie, where she could keep in touch with Bill Dalton and always know what was going on with the lawmen. Ransom Payne got to the ranch an hour after we left, she learned, late as usual. He never got any closer to the gang. He was one miserable cowardly Marshal.

Old Man Mundy had money and was a good businessman, and Flo worked him for all she could. He didn't have much left for the bed, and when Flo wasn't ridin' off on one excuse or another to Greer County she was with me. I was a stable hand, not quite an hostler and not quite a boss in a place near the butcher shop. I had a private room for myself and enough pay to leave me keep my stake intact. It was a real nice winter and springtime. The man that owned the stable was friendly to the Daltons, and no Marshal ever came close to knowin' who I was, although I had to hide from Hi Semple a couple times when the O-Bar-Z owner was on a bender in Guthrie. It was a quiet time, although the Daltons and all the gang fretted over it a lot. Bob and Grat stayed mainly drunk and the others stole a few horses but never did get into the papers, exceptin' for somethin' they didn't do. Bob liked to read the stories anyway. Long as they spelled his name right he loved it.

♞

YOU GOT TO REMEMBER THAT BY 18 and 92 the country was fillin' up. All kinds of people come into the Border States and the Territory. There was telephones and everything. Railroads crisscrossed the entire countryside. The more people the more law, the more business, the more brains lookin' for a way to make a dollar. It was bad times for outlaws.

Take this Chris Madsen. He was a Scandahoovian who had come to the U.S. and A. and joined the army and learned the language—though he always spoke with a funny accent—and had been with Custer but had sense enough not to be at Little Big Horn, although there was some who said he had and got away, which he didn't. He was lawsmart. He knew the Daltons were gettin' information from the poor folks and from Flo and from Bill Dalton, too. But he wasn't like Ransom Payne ridin' around and hollerin' and tryin' to bully people. He began to work from inside. He began to get the people who didn't like the Daltons to talk, and he began cozenin' them who did. He was the dangerous lawman and both Flo and Bill knew it.

Which was why on June 1st in 18 and 92 Bill Dalton sat with the Federal judge and the Federal prosecutor at ten o'clock of the night. The bunch of us were at Red Rock.

Flo had set it up all over again. Not that she didn't know all about Madsen and his setup with the other lawmen; not that she didn't see things clear as crystal—it was her one blind spot to believe they could make that one big strike and quit the business. We talked about it in my room at the livery stable. She had acted nervous and upset and had yanked me into the bed for a couple of hours before she calmed down.

She said, "What with Bob drunk and that old man no good, I don't know what I'd do without you, Timothy. Maybe you hadn't ought to go with them to Red Rock."

"If I don't I'll have to take off. You know how they are. They think I'm good luck since last time."

"How's your bank account?"

"Better than theirs. Or yours." I had it in a belt, which I slept in. "You need somethin' for yourself?"

"Never from you." She was naked on the bed, smiling at me in that wonderful way she had. "When we make the big one and it all ends I want you to be well heeled and ready to go."

"You been awful good to me, Flo. I wish things was different, somehow."

"Do you?"

"I wish . . ." I couldn't tell her.

She said, "Timothy, I am twenty-two years old. The same age as Bob. I've been cattin' around since I was twelve. Don't think of me that way."

"What way?" I had never heard her talk like that.

"You know what way. I'm tied to Bob. Sometimes I wonder why, sometimes I think I'll quit. But we've been together off and on for a long while. It's like a partnership, and he needs me a lot worse'n I need him. Maybe if you were older . . . Hell, no, what am I talkin' about? I wouldn't be any good to any one man except Bob. He understands me."

I almost told her I was twenty—I had passed my fifteenth birthday and growed to be bigger than Bob, as big as Grat and a hell of a lot stronger, workin' the way I did, drinkin' little, keepin' steady hours. Not to say gettin' plenty from Flo, which kept me out of bad company.

I said, "How much you figure to get this time?"

"Bill says over fifty thousand."

"You reckon Bob'll give the boys another bad count, like last time?"

"If he can get away with it. I must say I'm against that,

always was. The Daltons think they're entitled, but Doolin and the others think different and Doolin could be rough."

"I always heard there was honesty among thieves. It ain't true. Sometimes it seems to me nothin' is true, not complete. The only person I can believe in is you."

I was standing alongside the bed lookin' down at her. She blinked a little, then reached out and took hold of me and said, "Honey, you come right down here and be loved." Then she laughed a little and said, "Only would you mind taking off that money belt?"

Well, she had come in and been in such a state and in such a hurry and I was so used to not takin' it off that I had plumb forgot. I had to laugh, too. She was always makin' funnies and we laughed a lot together.

So there I was holdin' the horses at Red Rock on the Otoe reservation in the night of June 1st and here come the train, zoomin' along on the tracks of the Santa Fe. It was lightnin' but not raining. There was Bob, Emmett and Grat and Doolin, Broadwell, Powers and Bitter Creek—the biggest bunch ever for that gang. Grat was so high on booze and his big first chance that he was droolin' and playin' with his gun.

Bob always watched Grat. The Daltons were not very bright, but everybody knew the eldest was a numbskull. Bob reined in close to him.

"Take it easy, big brother. And leave that hawgleg alone. We don't shoot people, we just rob 'em."

"I'd admire to shoot me a trainman. I'd purely love to see one of them bastards bleed."

"Don't you try it."

"If you say, Bob. But it gripes me, the way they

hounded me."

"Just be happy with the loot," Bob said.

The others were placed like before. You seen one train robbery you seen them all, no use to go into it. But this time there was a difference. When the train slowed down I saw it, and give Bob credit, he spotted it also.

He yelled, "Look at that dark coach behind the express car. Hold everything, boys."

Grat said, "The hell with it. What the hell you scared of?"

"Bein' bushwhacked," Bob said so all could hear.

"Damn right," Doolin hollered. "Everybody lay off."

Bob yanked the reins of Grat's horse and they pulled back to where I was holdin' for the others. They came in afoot, using all the cuss words in the book. Grat was cryin' real tears and usin' the worst language of all.

Bob tried to shut them up. "Flo warned me. Madsen is gettin' too goddam smart."

I spoke up. "She also said to stick around if this happened. Might be there's another train behind. Might be it's carryin' the express money."

"Timothy's right," said Bob.

They waited. It was about the only time Bob ever followed Flo's notions to the letter. The long layoff, the reports from Bill and her and me had made him a bit careful for that time anyway. He had some bit of brains, more than any of them but Bill, who was about even with him and a lot slicker. Not that Bill was a coward, he was just sneaky smart.

It was real weird out there with the lightning flashin' and no sound except those of the saddles creakin' and bridles rattlin' and Grat mumblin' curses and the night insects and maybe a bird or two flappin' its wings or makin' a night call.

Then we heard the hummin' of the cars on the rails. The boys all brightened up and Grat let out a long rebel yell. They formed up and Grat insisted on taking the engineer along with Bob.

"But don't shoot, damn it," Bob said.

The train slowed down and the brothers rode in alongside shootin' into the air and jumped aboard. I gathered the horses and the train stopped. Bob jumped down and made for the express car. Shots rang out, and it wasn't all the Dalton gang.

The first train had been a decoy, all right, and now it looked like there was a posse on the second one. The horses plunged and I had to pull them back, using a drag line through the bridles, which I had sorta invented to hold that many of 'em. Our bunch was firin' wild in the dark, but in a flash of lightnin' I saw something. I tried to get in to Bob but couldn't leave the horses, so I dragged them along 'til I was near enough to make him hear.

He said, "What the hell?"

"It's all comin' from the express car," I told him. "Looks like two men with several guns, maybe."

"Right," he said and moved around, and then everybody in the gang concentrated on the express car. In a minute the firin' from there stopped and the messenger and a guard got down with their hands up, shakin' in their boots when they realized what might happen to them, cringin' when they saw Grat, with his dumb, fierce face and his big pistol glarin' at them.

But Bob merely told them to open the safe. The messenger was still playing hero and tried to say he couldn't since he didn't have the combination. Bill Doolin grabbed a sledge hammer standin' in a corner of the car and went to work smashing at the door and the safe flew open. Emmett was in the car by then and he picked up the sledge and beat on several cases of merchandise. They busted and there was all kinds of female flummery, dresses and underwear and all.

Doolin and Bob went for the cash. Emmett began handing down bundles of the stuff for the girls. They were laughing and having a real ball. The passengers were scared, held under the guns of the rest of the bunch. It wasn't much of an excitement. They bundled up everything and came for the horses and away we went into the night.

Once more Bob had managed to get hold of the loot, but this time Doolin stayed with him and never took his eyes off the sack. We rode hard and fast into the Otoe reservation.

Bob and Grat had been lawmen only a few years ago in this dark, thickly wooded country, and they knew each highway and byway. We traveled mainly the byways, through thickets, forests, avoiding any human life, scaring up small animals, pushing hard for a place the Daltons knew. It was an all-night push and both horses and men were exhausted when we came to a clearing at dawn.

But Bill Doolin was not too worn out to keep his gaze fixed on Bob. He was alone and everyone knew it—these were all Dalton people. Bitter Creek, Broadwell, Powers had been cheated before and had done nothing about it. Doolin walked with Bob, six feet from him, his gunbelt shifted so that he could make a play if he had to. He had grown up a lot since we had seen him last, and maybe Bob recognized this.

Doolin said, "Just empty it on the ground, Bob."

"Why, sure. What else?" Bob held the sack by its corners and looked around. Nobody said anything.

"I want to see it done," Doolin told him.

"What the hell's with him?" demanded Grat. He had a bottle and was swigging from it pretty good.

"Ask them," Doolin said, pointing to the others who had been shorted the last time they had robbed a train.

Bob said, "The past is the past, Bill." He up-ended the sack. There was a lot of currency and a heap of stiff-paper certificates in bundles tied separately. "Ought to be fifty thousand here."

Doolin picked up one of the bundles, making sure everyone saw his move. He peered at them in the morning light.

"Yeah," he said. "These here are non-negotiable."

"They are what?" asked Grat. "What the hell you talkin' about?"

Doolin said, "Any good thief has got to know if what he steals is worth anything." He picked up another bundle. "These bankers and people are gettin' too goddam smart. You got to identify yourself and countersign and all sorts of shit in order to cash these here securities. All of 'em. Ask Bob."

Bob examined the stock certificates and bank draughts. His face grew long and turned red. "Sonofabitch. Bill's right."

"Count the cash," said Emmett. "Let's see what we did get. Hell, it ain't even good wages for the last months."

Bob was counting the cash money. Doolin squatted beside him but both were so disheartened they weren't much interested.

Bob said, "I make it about eight hundred apiece. Okay, Bill?"

"What about the kid?"

"Two hundred," said Bob. "See here?"

"Okay, Timothy?" asked Doolin.

I took the bills and stuck them in my pocket, not wanting them to know about the money belt, in which I now had more than each had taken from the train. "Sure, that's okay."

"You're a good kid," said Doolin. "I be damn, this is gettin' to be a stinkin' business we're in."

Bob said, "Flo was countin' on them securities."

"She coulda been right. Like I say, they're gettin' too hi-falutin' in the business world today." Doolin stretched. "Reckon we better split up here?"

"We better lead you out of the reservation. Them Indian police can be real tough," Bob said. "Then we'll split. Flo and Bill will have to go back to work. I still say we got to get lucky just one time. Hell, if Jesse and the Youngers could do it, we can do it. I aim to beat Jesse before I'm through."

"We're gettin' our names in the papers as often as he did," Emmett said. He and Bob, they were always comparin' us to the James gang.

"There's more newspapers today," said Doolin. "And they got fewer of us to write about. I dunno. I ain't for goin' back to work nohow, but this is plumb discouragin'."

He spoke for them all. We got on our horses and the rest of the ride wasn't happy, exceptin' for Grat. He had his bottle and he hadn't seen any coin in so long that eight hundred was a fortune to him. He could buy a lot of rotgut booze and sleazy women for that, he figured.

Meantime Grat and Emmett were on their way to see

Mama Dalton when we split. Bob and me headed for Guthrie. I had asked for time off to visit folks I didn't have—but there were so many Youngers the boss believed me—and Bob was to meet Flo and go on to Greer County.

He said to me, "It's sure hell not to find as much as we expect in them express cars. But robbin' the passengers don't bring much and it makes people mad at us. The business sure is gettin' rough."

"Flo would like to quit."

"Sure she would. She's got that notion about Mexico, and prob'ly she's right. But I mean to make a name for us before I quit. I mean to make us the biggest ever operated."

"I know, Bob." I'd heard it often enough.

"A man's put in this world, he's got to go his way. If he's a real man he wants to make his mark."

"Well, sure."

"You wasn't with us at the start but you know we didn't start out to rob trains. We was lawmen. My brother Frank got what a lawman gets—no pay and shot to death. Then they turned agin me and Grat. We was forced to hit the trail."

"Uh-huh." It was a damn big lie but I guess Bob believed it. Truth was, they were drunks and lazy and they didn't mind killin' other people to make a dollar. They had killed one fella for stealin' Bob's girl—that was before he met Flo Quick. Truth was, the Dalton gang was all a bunch of nogoods any way you looked at 'em. If it wasn't for Flo they'd all be dead or in jail by then.

"Well, we proved we're the best damn train robbers alive. No question about it. The papers all say so."

"Yea, that's right."

"I got to figure out somethin'. Flo and Bill, they've been

wrong too often about the size of the haul we could make. I got to figure out somethin'. Grat, he's plain dumb. Emmett, he's just a kid. Doolin, he's allus got ideas but they're no good. It's up to me—the rest of 'em are just plain work hands."

"That's right." It was no use arguin' with him, even when he was sober. He was plain headstrong.

"You stick with me, Timothy, I'll make you famous."

He went on like that for two days, and at night we come to the outskirts of Guthrie. I was plain weary of listenin' to him, but all the Daltons was always big talkers.

I said, "Uh, Bob, how about we go in separate? Meet me at the stable?"

"That's smart, boy. Then they can't bag two of us."

That's the way he was, playin' the big leader. He didn't give a damn about me, but he knew I wasn't a shooter and wouldn't be any good to him in a fight. So he acted out his part like he was on the stage. We parted and I rode straight in to the stable. I went into my room the back way without anybody seein' me—and there was Flo, and once again she was upset, only this time she was madder'n a wet hen.

I said, "What happened?"

"That fool Ransom Payne. While you were robbin' the train he was comin' in on us in Texas. Oh, I was tipped off, I got my trunk down in a stall. But just to have him, of all people, find our place, it makes me screamin' sore."

I said, "Bob's on his way, be here in a minute or two."

"How much did you get?"

"Not enough." I told her about the securities.

She said, "You mean they didn't find the express box?"

"What express box?"

"Oh, hell. I might have known. The express box was full of cash and securities we could collect on. Oh, dear, when will they ever learn? I told them."

I said, "Bob's got some pretty dresses and stuff. Emmett found it."

"Sure, gewgaws. But not the express box." She dropped onto my chair and stared at the wall. "And now we got to find another hideout. With eight hundred dollars. Well, the hell with Bob. I know a spot for him and his dumb brothers. I'm staying here. Old Man Mundy hasn't quite had enough of me."

"But you had enough of him."

"It don't matter." She shook herself and a grim expression came over her face. "Let's go downstairs."

Just as we got into the yard Bob rode up. He jumped down and threw his arms around Flo and she pushed him away, acting real excited and worried.

"You've got to go. Right now."

"Don't you wanta hear about it all? Don't you want some money?"

"You'll need it all. Madsen and Thomas and just about every Marshal is on the hunt. The telegraph was humming. There'll be a hundred lawmen on the trail."

"But what about our place?"

"Ransom Payne," she said. "You go warn your brothers and the others. You'll be doing some riding, Bob. You haven't got a minute to spare."

"Is it that bad?"

"Worse," she said. "Bill's got an alibi, but they're watching him now. We'll be in touch. We'll send the word through the underground when it's safe."

He said, "Well, hell, Flo . . ."

"You'd better hurry, Bob."

"Well, if you say so." He kissed her again and jumped on his horse. He said, "Timothy, you look after her, you hear?"

"You bet, Bob."

He rode out. She turned and stared at me.

"That's the first time I ever sent him on his way without any lovin'."

"Well, if it's as bad as all that . . ."

"It is. But we could have . . . I'm just fed up, Timothy. I just couldn't stand it tonight."

I said, "You goin' to Mundy's?"

"And have that old goat creeping over me? No. I'm staying here. I'll leave early enough to not be noticed."

"Sure, Flo. I'll sleep down here in a stall."

She looked at me and laughed in a small way. "Timothy, I didn't say anything about a young goat creeping over me. You come upstairs this minute."

Funny part of it, Flo was right. Madsen and the rest really were out, and there was much more than a hundred in the posses after the Daltons. A new man named Swayne was a terrier—he was the last to give up as the Gang retreated to the deepest boondocks, rode into Kansas, Texas, anywhere to escape. Bob must've been real happy the way the newspapers played it up all over the Border States country. Somebody told me it even got into the New York and Chicago papers.

Flo walked the streets in dresses up to her chin and down to the streets and high-laced boots and little hats, and nobody noticed her. Bill Dalton sneaked in after a couple weeks and we all sat in my room.

"Damn, they're keepin' watch on me," he said. "You got anything?"

"Adair," she told him. "Check it out. It's a good spot and near the Neosho. I think maybe mid-July there'll be a big shipment."

"I can find out. But do you think it might be too soon?"

"They won't expect it. The bunch has kept low, and Bob sent word they're anxious and ready. Missing that express box at Red Rock—they're runnin' out of money, of course."

Bill said, "Sometimes those brothers of mine are so damn dumb I could disown 'em."

"I always hope the next one will be the last."

"Live in hopes, die in despair, my mama always says." Bill was lower'n a snake's belly. "Bein' a Dalton has about finished me in politics."

He was finished before he began if he only knew it. He didn't have the class, he looked like a dressed up bum always.

Flo said, "Well, I'm going for a new hideout just in case we strike it rich this time. We'll send word in the usual way."

"I'm gettin' worried about some of them people. We haven't had the money to grease them good enough."

"Just pick your grapevine," she told him. "That's your job. And find out which train is loaded."

"Okay," he said. He slunk out of there with his head wagging in all directions for fear a Marshal would be watching.

Flo said, "He's damn little better than the others."

"They're all a bunch of dummies." I'd said this a few times before. "You're wastin' your life on 'em."

"It might work at Adair."

No use to talk to her. Women always live in hopes, as Bill said. I was real worried she would really die in despair. She took off and I didn't see her around Guthrie and didn't know where she was for that time, and a good thing it was.

Because Chris Madsen dropped by the livery stable one day in the first week of July, 18 and 92, and scared the livin' wits outa me. He talked to my boss, then came to me in the stall where I was curryin' one of the rental horses.

He was a squatty man with pale eyes and a bushy mustache. He had a deep look, he could make you feel all thumbs. He stared at me a long while, then he spoke.

"Timothy Younger it is, yah?" He had this accent from Scandahoovia or wherever.

"Yah . . . I mean yes."

"Younger, dot is not a goot name in this part of the country."

"I ain't related," I said truthfully.

"Dot's goodt. You know a fella name of Bill Dalton?"

"That ain't a good name, neither." I knew I couldn't show him how scared I was. "But people know Bill, he's always politickin' around."

"Yah. So he been aroundt here?"

"Here? Why should he be around here?"

"It has been said."

"Well, if he has I wouldn't know about it. I'm only a stable boy. I ain't old enough to vote."

"You vasn't aroundt here last June first, vas you?"

"I dunno, wasn't I?"

"Vell, your boss says you was visitin' relatives. But not relatives to the Younger brothers, eh, vat?"

"Oh, sure. I was up in Missouri—in the Ozarks, you

know. Not even a town. Just a hill farm, some cousins I got up there."

"I see." He kept staring at me.

I said, "Goin' up there again pretty soon. There's a certain little old gal asked me to come back."

"Oh. A gal, yah?"

"Sort of a fifth cousin once removed. Pretty as a little speckled hen."

He lost interest. "Yah. Boys and girls. Yah. Okay. If you see Bill Dalton you report to me, Chris Madsen, yah?"

He talked like a comedy fella I saw on the stage with Flo one time, but he didn't look like one. He had no neck, just shoulders and a kind of big head and those cold eyes. He wore his hat straight on his head, and that was a funny thing because that's the way the Daltons wore their hats—never slanchwise, always straight. He had the cold, mean look of a lawman, Madsen did.

I said, "Well, sure, but I wouldn't know him anyways."

He went away. I waited until he was out of sight. Then I went to the telephone in the office of the boss. I wasn't supposed to use it but right now I didn't care. I was scared of it, of course, the newfangled damn thing, but I had a number and I gave it to the operator and she connected me.

"Bill Dalton here."

I said, "Timothy. Where's Bob?"

"Shhhh! Don't talk like that. I'll be right over."

"You better not. I'll meet you corner of Main and Oklahoma in about a half hour."

I went to my room and made a bedroll and buckled on my revolver and took my rifle out of its wrapping and went down and saddled up the sorrel. I didn't even see the boss, I just rode out. Kids were always takin' off for here and there in those days, and seein' as Madsen had been after me he would think I got scared or somethin', and truth to tell I didn't give a damn what he thought. I was long gone already.

Bill stood on the corner and I never did get down off the sorrel. I found out where Bob was at and that Flo had gone westward to Woodward, where she had folks. I rode right on out of Guthrie. I augured with myself whether to head for Woodward or to join Bob in his camp. It seemed to me that she was so tangled up with Bob that the best way was to go to him first.

On July 13th I was with Bob and the others, same bunch which had done the Red Rock job, on the bank of the Neosho between Pryor and Adair. They had a sort of jungle camp in the high-growin' brush along the river edge.

Bob was in no kind of humor. "Flo send me a message? Where you been, anyway?"

"I haven't seen Flo. Nobody offered me a message, I had to get it from Bill. Marshal Madsen was on me about Bill."

"You ain't seen Flo?"

"Nope."

"Where the hell is she?"

"I thought you'd know more about that than me."

"Damn her, she was supposed to. . . ." He stopped. "Well, she always turns up, that's for sure. Madsen, huh?"

"You bet. Mean as a snake."

"After Bill."

"That's right"

"I don't like it at all. Bill won't be no good to us any more if he's watched that close."

"That's what I figured. You reckon maybe he got onto Flo, too?" It had been worrying me all the way up to the Territory that Madsen was closin' in on all of us.

"Could be. If she took off that quick and quiet."

I said, "This time maybe it had better be Mexico, huh?"

"All accordin'," he said. He had a strange look about him. He'd been drinking—they was all always drinking—but he wasn't drunk, he was more like fanatic. "We had over a hundred chasin' us and we got away. They can't catch the Daltons. I reckon to make that big strike yet. We can't miss."

He had his own way of figurin' things. It seemed to me that the small haul they had made and the big chase would have been a warning that they were on the downgrade. He never could see it thataway. Never. It just wasn't in him, nor Grat nor Emmett neither. Bill saw it, I'm certain, but the riders never could see it.

None of the others seen it, neither. Doolin was gettin' sick of the small hauls and bein' bossed by Bob, but he always thought it could be done, that the railroads were there to be robbed by men like him. Broadwell and Powers believed in the Daltons. Bitter Creek was such a dummy he didn't know anything from doodley-squat. Further and more their luck was runnin' out, and this was something they couldn't know even if they were smart.

The information they had was that the train they wanted was comin' through on July 15th. The way they got the inside dope was from railway employees who were sore at their bosses for one reason or another and could be pumped by Flo or Bill. This time it was Bill who got the tipoff. It was that afternoon that two men came stumblin' into the camp lookin' for strayed horses.

One of the men asked, "You boys campin' here?"

"Just passin' through," Bob told him, blocking off Grat, who was going for his gun to shoot any possible witnesses.

"Well, sure. We'll be on our way." But they looked back and we could see them talkin' to each other and it was possible they would be runnin' to the law. This country had filled up since the days when the Daltons had been law officers. There was too many who would listen to a story about armed men so near the rails.

Doolin said, "They'll have the town in an uproar."

Of all, the least expected agreed. Grat said, "Bill's right. This here is another bust. I feel it in my bones."

I thought they were right, and Bob was grim for a few minutes. If there was a posse waitin' for us at Pryor we couldn't hit between there and Adair, the next town, like it was planned. In a while Bob brightened up.

"All right. Pryor's expectin' us, let's say. Saddle up. We're ridin' west."

"To whereabouts?" asked Doolin.

"To Adair, that's where. We were goin' to hit there in the first place, right? Then it looked better here. So now we go back to our first notion."

"But they might telegraph to Adair."

"Then get a hustle on," Bob said. "What's the matter, youall scared?"

They were too dumb to be scared. They were more afraid somebody would think they were scared. We rode for Adair.

It was about nine-thirty when Bob had it lined up—a new scheme, something we had not done before. I took care of the horses like always. The town lay sleepy some distance from the tracks and there was only the station agent in the depot.

Bob and Grat stuck their guns into the depot and the agent near upchucked his dinner. There was a safe and some money from fares and freight and stuff, which made Grat real happy. They tied up the agent and gagged him.

There were no passengers waiting so they all went into the station and sat around waiting for the 9:42, a passenger train, one of the prides of the Katy down here. There was a few loungers around the platform but they didn't pay attention, thinkin' the Gang was a bunch of riders waitin' to take the train.

It was right on time, 9:42. The Gang came out of the depot and Bitter Creek held the loungers easy with his rifle. Grat and Emmett waited until the train screeched down to a halt and jumped the engineer and fireman. Bob made for the express car like always, with Broadwell and Powers sidin' him, and like always the messenger made his play at not givin' up.

I saw four of the passengers run and dive into a coal shed beside the track but thought nothin' of it. Passengers have done strange things during a train robbery, you wouldn't believe some of them.

Bob yelled at the messenger, "We got plenty of dynamite here. You want to get blown up?"

The messenger was stubborn. Then all of a sudden there was this burst of gunfire from the coal shed. Them four hadn't been ordinary passengers, that was for sure.

The gang just wheeled around and began shooting back. They had the advantage of being scattered, while the ones in the coal shed were bunched. Now the passengers really did duck under seats, behind each other, anything to keep out of the way of a stray bullet. Away from the tracks, on the edge of town, two men were havin' coffee and mindin' their own business. Turned out they was the only two doctors Adair had. Damned if wild shots didn't go right through the thin old frame walls of the drug store and knock down both of them. Lead was really flyin', and I was usin' the horses for cover even as I managed to get them as far out of the line of fire as possible.

After a while there was no more gunfire from the shed. The Daltons had always been good shots, and the concentrated fire had taken care of the four men. One of them kept hollerin' for somebody to come out and help them from the cars. After a minute I made out he was yellin' for Marshal Ransom Payne. That was a laugher. Payne was not about to do battle. Through the car windows I finally spotted him and some other fellas wearin' stars. They were all squinched down with their guns drawn but not comin' to the party. They was some bunch of lawmen.

Grat was gettin' wild as usual. He climbed on the roof of the express car and found a ventilator and shoved the muzzle of his sixshooter into it and pulled the trigger. Then he emptied his rifle. That much lead bouncin' around and ricochetin' was too much for the messenger. He opened the door to the car.

Bob was as mad as I've ever seen him, what with the gunfight and the messenger holdin' up the parade, and he scared the fella into openin' the safe. They grabbed all they could find and put it in the usual wheat sack. There was no express box this time, like the one they had missed at Red Rock.

Officers on the train, no express box—the signs were all bad. The bunch fired several shots over the heads of everyone in sight and came for the horses. I had them all lined up and ready. One more bullet came singin' through the night and clipped my hat brim. It made a nick but I grabbed and held onto the hat and my sorrel was off and runnin' ahead of them all.

This time Bob figured on bein' chased by more than one posse. He led us into country where we had never been before. He took us up and down streams and into hills. When the hour of the split arrived and the sun had come up enough to give us some light to divvy by, we were on top of a knoll where we could see in all directions and spot anybody chasin' us.

It was a misty morning and the light was poor. The gang looked beat and put down by the hard ride. There wasn't any air of great expectation like before. The shootin' and all that seemed to have shrunk them—they didn't stand so tall. Nobody said anything, they just stood around or hunkered down while Bob emptied the sack. It was like they knew this hadn't been the big hit. It was almost like they had knowed it all the time.

Bob said, "I be damn. It's just about what we got last time. I be double damn."

"The business has gone to hell," Doolin said.

Nobody disagreed, even Grat, who was at his bottle like always. They all took their cut. Bob give me another two hundred and I took it and kept my mouth shut.

Doolin said, "Kid, you deserve more. It ain't easy holdin' the cavvy like you did."

"It's all right," I said. "I got to agree with you, the business is gone to hell."

"He don't know his ass from his elbow about nothin'," said Bitter Creek. "My Rose is gonna raise hell about this.

She wants to go to Mexico with Bob and Flo and Emmett and Julia."

"Women," said Grat. "Whole trouble is with the goddam women. If you bastards would use whores we'd all be better off."

"Oh, shut up, Grat," said Emmett. "You're such a hog you wouldn't know about decent women."

"Decent?" Grat haw-hawed. "Flo Quick? That lil old monkey-fuckin' Rose Dunn? Sheee-it."

Bitter Creek jumped up. "All right. That fixes it for me. I allus was with you, Bob, now wasn't I? Sided you all the way. But I don't have to put up with your dirty-mouth brother. You can forget about me. I'll go some place. Me and Rose. I've done had all I can take from him."

He ran to his horse. I was truly surprised—I didn't think he ever had a thought Bob didn't give him. He did hesitate for a minute, and I reckon if Bob had said something he would've stayed. But Bob was as down-hearted as the rest, and Bitter Creek rode away and that's the last I ever seen of him and no loss, either, in my mind.

The downgrade had started at Red Rock with the small amount of loot and the hard chase afterwards. Now the gang was bustin' up.

Bob said, "Well . . . the grapevine has showed a lot of holes. Flo and Bill done what they could but what the hell, you can see it ain't workin' right. Let's split up and I'll think of somethin'."

Doolin said, "Count me out. I ain't sayin' I quit the business, but I don't like some things and we sure ain't gettin' nowhere."

"Okay, Bill. No hard feelins?" Bob stared at him.

"No hard feelins. Hell, I ain't got sense enough to hold grudges," Doolin said, grinning at us all. "We had some fun together. Good luck to yawl."

He rode out. Powers and Broadwell said nothing, but they stuck, and Grat was at his bottle, not carin' a damn for anything.

"Good riddance," Grat said. "You'll think of somethin', Bob. You always did."

"Sure he will," said Emmett. "Nobody can beat the Daltons when it comes down to the nub."

Bob said, "Well, yawl better get on. Bill, Dick, you know where to go. Me and Grat and Emmett, we got to see Mama, then we will hole up and ponder a bit. We'll get word to you."

They left. Bob looked at me.

"I dunno what to do about you, Timothy. Guthrie ain't no place for you with Madsen on your back."

"I better look for Flo, hadn't I?"

"She'll be in touch. You wanta ride with us?" It was a half-hearted offer. Of course, he didn't know that I could find Flo real easy, and I wasn't about to tell him. Her leavin' off like she did and the way she'd been actin' lately, I figured it was better I talked to her alone and away from him.

"No, you got your own business to attend to."

"Flo's entitled to a cut from this here job but it ain't much. She won't like that."

"I wouldn't know."

"Well, you go ahead. We'll get word around when we need you again."

"Okay. So-long, then."

I turned the nose of the sorrel westward. It was a long

ride to Woodward and then I had to find Flo, and it wouldn't take long for Bob to learn where she was. The grapevine was beginnin' to shred a bit, but it wasn't altogether tore loose. There were plenty of poor folk who would think the Adair robbery was a fine thing against the railroads they purely hated.

But as I rode I went back over what had happened and how it had happened, and all the signs was plain as the nose on your face. The time for the Daltons was gone. Just about everybody in the Border States and the Territory knew 'em by sight. The Post Offices had their mugs on the wall. Madsen was a methodical and smart man and he was puttin' an awful lot of time on them. They was good riders and good shots, but they couldn't see the way things had changed and they couldn't get Jesse and the Youngers out of their thick skulls. Hell, Jesse'd been dead since 18 and 83, and with him the freebootin' times had gone.

At the livery stable the boss took the papers and some magazines, like *Leslie's*, and all you had to do was read them and you could see what was happenin'. Farmers and factories, and in the far west the railroads and mining and the big ranchers, had taken over. There was as many churches as saloons, exceptin' in the big cities like New York and Chicago. The Barbary Coast was tamed, Billy the Kid and them were all dead, and Bill Cody was runnin' a horse and Indian circus. It just wasn't any time to be holdin' up trains; the telephone and telegraph had you nailed down in a jiffy. Only the Daltons could ignore all these things.

Ridin' easy to save the sorrel gave me a lot of time to think. At fifteen years of age, with money in your belt, you got the notion you're the boss of yourself and what happens to you. It takes some years to find out nobody ain't the captain of his soul. There's a bunch of luck goes into it all, and maybe somethin' higher, I ain't just sure. But I did know that ridin' with the Daltons wasn't somethin' wild and good and helpful for the future of Timothy Younger.

♘

As soon as I came to the farm in Woodward I knew a lot more about Florence Quick. It was a place that nobody would pick to farm. It was also rundown and tacky wherever you looked. The house was needin' paint and the barn never did have any. The crops looked poorly and neglected.

Her folks matched the surroundings. Her ma might've been pretty but she was all washed out, grey-colored and skinnied down to a shadow. Her pa looked like he had fought a losin' battle from birth. They were little people no matter how you looked at them. They stared at you suspicious and they never smiled and they seldom had anything to say except "pass the pertaters." It was no wonder Flo had to run away and stay away from such people.

It seemed I was spendin' my early life in stables, and maybe that's where I belonged, but it took me two days to clean up and get out the worst of the rats as big as terriers and make a sleepin' place for myself and a decent stall for the sorrel. Flo helped me, talkin' all the time, once more nervous as a cat in a dog kennel. We had a couple quick ones in the haymow, but her folks were real oldtime religious and we had to be careful. She wasn't the old Flo in many ways, although she claimed it was because we had to hurry so—she was a gal that liked to take her time.

She said, "You see how it is? There's no place for me.

No place at all."

"You got any plans for the Gang?"

"Absolutely none."

"Are you finished with Bob?"

Her fingernails were already bit to pieces. She chewed on a thumb. "I can't say that. When the message comes I'll go to him. He's the nearest thing . . . well, exceptin' you, Timothy. Without you, I don't know. But when he calls I'll go and listen to him. He's bound to have something."

"I think they all know the train dodge is finished."

"I know it. You know it. For that matter Doolin must know it, but Bill's a funny one."

"Bob's got Grat, Emmett, Powers and Broadwell."

"And us."

"Well, I dunno."

"If I go will you go with me?"

There was only one answer to that. "What else? But I still got that stake to start for California."

"You're sweet. You're my rock."

She backed up against the bales of hay in the barn and we went at it again. I never could get enough of that woman. She was sweet as sugar and willing and warm, and what else was there to compare to her? Nothin', that's what.

Later she said, "Bob and Emmett, always talking about Jesse James. You know, in a way they're better men? Jesse shot people for no reason time and again. The Daltons are not killers like that oldtime crowd."

"They also ain't that smart."

"Well, no. They're not that smart. In fact they're pretty unsmart. But maybe Bob will come up with something. Banks—I've been thinking about banks. That's where they keep the money, after all."

"They guard it pretty good, too."

"Timothy, sometimes I think you haven't got robber's blood."

"Been thinkin' a lot about that myself lately. I know I ain't got killer blood."

"Killing is wasteful and dangerous," she said like a schoolmarm pronouncin' a solid fact, not to be denied. "I have told that to the Gang time and time again. Grat, he's the only killer in the whole crowd. And Bob controls Grat drunk or sober."

"The day'll come when Grat's too drunk or too dumb," I said. "I hope we never hear from 'em."

August came in and I worked the farm as best I could. Flo got restless and we took a ride and came back with some horses we had sort of found, some real good stock. The idea was for Dan Quick to start a herd for himself, but he had no knack for horses. He ran a few head of cattle, so we took another ride and brought him in some prime beef, and that brought us to September, a real nice month, warm and balmy. We dammed up a creek on the back of the property and made a swimmin' hole, and Ma Quick thought that it was a sin to bathe in public. She should of seen Flo and me skinny dippin' under the moon when the folks was asleep.

Word came. Bob had a notion. He would need horses and he would need some money for this and that. In other words, the Daltons had spent all they had and were hollerin' once more for Flo to bail 'em out.

I was dead against it. I argued and argued. It wasn't any good. She had that loyalty to Bob. She pointed out that her old man couldn't handle the string we had stole and why shouldn't we drive them over and give 'em to Bob?

There was no use. We left at night so as not to answer any questions. Each of us put twenty dollars on the kitchen table before we took off. We only drove out five of the best horses besides my sorrel and a fine bay pony Flo favored.

She had herself all dressed up in a divided skirt and shiny boots and a long-sleeved man's western-type shirt and a little tight hat. She looked a real lady. We were to pose as aunt and nephew going to join uncle in Guthrie. For a laugh we used the name of "Mundy," her old man butcher.

We camped where it was pleasant, and when the rains came we stopped at wayside inns. It was great fun to see her lord it over some innkeeper, spending money, drinking wine or beer, treatin' me like I was a kid, always makin' people like her and want to talk with her.

In one of the places it got pretty rough. There was a big cattleman from Texas took a shine to her, and she was maybe a little too nice to him. Anyway, she was asleep when he came pushin' at her door.

She didn't want that kind of notoriety, not at that time. She knocked on the wall and I come awake and listened. She let the cattleman in. It was midnight and we'd only had a couple hours sleep. I heard her connin' this galoot and got dressed and the bedroll ready, figurin' what was goin' to happen. I tippy-toed to her door and waited.

I heard him say, "Hey, now, lady, just a minute."

Then I busted in. She had her revolver in her hand. He had his pants at half mast. I put my gun on him and she began to dress.

I said, "Don't bother to raise your hands, mister. Just hang onto your pants."

"I thought you were a gent," she said to him. She was full of fire. "I never believed you would misunderstand a lady."

"I'm plumb sorry, Mrs. Mundy," he said. "You don't have to point that thang at me, young fella. I'll go peaceable. Just made a mistake, that's all. Too much firewater."

"You don't trust him," she said. "Make him lay down on the bed."

"Face in the pillow," I told him. "This here gun is on a hair trigger."

He flopped down, a big hunk of a man. It was real funny. Flo was dressed and packed in a moment or two. She went over to the bed and dug into the man's pockets so quick he didn't even know what happened. She came up with a poke that was fat and sassy.

She said, "I refuse to stay under the same roof with such a man. Timothy, you get the horses ready. We'll just go on into the night."

"You don't have to do that, honest," he said. "I'll be good, I promise."

"You'll be good, all right."

I was already going down the back stairs. I rounded up the string and saddled our horses and there she came, laughin' and runnin'. We got out of there like a couple of rabbits and we rode hard that night and all the next day. There was over a hundred dollars in the Texan's poke, which we spent freely as we headed for the encampment where Bob waited for us. She had locked the big man in her room and we always wondered how he got out of it and if he had to explain how he got there in the first place. It was always a heap of fun and games ridin' with Flo Quick, believe me.

Part of what we spent the Texan's money on was clothing

for the boys. One of our informers had told us they wasn't lookin' too good, and if there was anything Flo hated it was seedy men. She knew all their sizes but Grat's, and we just bought big shirts and long pants for him and a couple different hat sizes . . . I was for skippin' him, but Flo refused to leave anyone out. She made it like it was Christmas or somethin' and us all a big family gettin' together. Her spirits grew higher and higher as we came closer to the place where we were to meet in northern Oklahoma not far from the Kansas line, down below Coffeyville, where the Daltons had more or less been raised up.

They come runnin' to us. We was the baggage train arrivin' in time to save the starvin' troops, all right. Flo had bought baskets of food-tinned fruit and tomatoes and sardines and stuff and loaves of bread and all kinds of stuff. They fell on it like they was starvin', and they looked it, all dirty and unshaven and their clothes in bad shape, even their boots and hats, which is the last thing they would allow to go down.

Bob said, "By God, it's good to see yawl. They been runnin' us around real pretty, them bastards."

"You look it," Flo said. She pushed Bob away. "Now every last one of you get down to the crick and bathe. Here's soap and towels and everything."

"It ain't hardly worth washin' to put back these here clothes," said Bob. "I tell you they been on our tails."

She began unpackin' bundles from the horse we had used to tote it all. "Get your tails clean and put on these duds. Come on, pick your styles, boys—something for everyone."

Well, they sure were like kids at a Christmas party. Outlaws, tough riders, all that—their daubers had been down, and now came help and they fairly leaped with joy. They selected their clothing and ran down to the nearby stream and stripped. I went with them, bein' dusty from the ride, and Flo went upstream with Bob's arm around her for their time together, out of sight around a bend.

We had also brought some booze, and I sat around with Emmett and Grat and Broadwell and Powers. They were real mysterious but they let me know Bob had a big plan and that they were all excited about it. They looked over the horses and pronounced them first rate. The one thing they had hung onto was their fancy saddles and their guns, and now they felt fully equipped and ready for anything. To me they seemed childish, the way they acted over every little thing. They were all young, but they were older than me and it was strange that I should feel older.

Flo and Bob was gone a long time, and I knew they had been talkin' because Bob never was that good with a woman. When they showed she was solemn and drawn again like she had been when I found her in Woodward. He was higher than a kite and went right to the whiskey, takin' it away from Grat.

He said, "Boys, Flo don't think much of our plan."

"I don't think a damn bit of it," she snapped. "It's the damnedest fool thing I ever heard of."

"I tell you I'm gonna top Jesse. I'm seein' his best play and I'm raisin' him." Bob took a big drink and grinned like a Halloween pumpkin.

"You betcha," said Grat. "No woman could think up a job like this. Nossir."

She gave him a long hard stare. "You can bet those new duds I bought for you that this woman wouldn't."

"It'll work and it'll make us famous," Emmett said. "I'm surprised you don't go along, Flo."

"Your own brother Bill don't go along." She was storming at them. "Bill Doolin don't go along. Nobody with a grain of sense in his head would go along."

Bob said, "Now wait a minute. There's Timothy. We all know he's a smart kid. Let's see what he has to say."

"Yes. See what Timothy thinks," said Flo. "Go ahead."

Bob was beaming like he had just discovered gold. "It's like this, Timothy. You know Coffeyville real good. You'll know that I'm right."

"Coffeyville?" I goggled at him. "Why you boys was practically raised there."

"And we know the town. Rode in a couple days ago and got a jug of alcohol from the druggist. Checked around to make sure I had everything down pat. You know the banks?"

"Banks? The two banks?"

"Right. Across the street from one another, right?"

"Well, sure."

"Handy, ain't it?"

"Handy for what?"

"Why for anybody with the guts to take 'em."

"Both banks? You got to rob both banks?"

"It beats anything Jesse ever did."

I said, "Jesse James had too much sense to try and hit two banks at once. Besides, everybody in Coffeyville knows you boys."

"A lot of good that'll do them chicken-shits," said Grat. He was posing around in his new clothes, suckin' on the bottle.

Broadwell, who seldom said anything, piped up. "From what the boys say there will be no problem with Coffeyville people. It was a tough town once; now it is tamed."

"That Marshal they got, Charlie Connolly, he don't even tote a gun," Bob said. "I tell you this is a lead-pipe cinch."

"Supposin' Madsen or somebody gets information," I said.

"Nobody knows exceptin' us."

"Just you boys? Five of you against a town? It ain't reasonable," I told him. "You asked me. I'm flat against it."

"Six of us," Bob said.

"Not me. Count me out. I got a yella streak," I said.

"Timothy's right. You can't go in there against two banks. Maybe one bank, but I'd have to check it out," Flo said. "It would take a lot of planning."

Grat pointed a finger at her. "You done your plannin'. What did we get? Peanuts. No more women. Us Daltons do this by our own selves."

"There are thirty-five hundred people in Coffeyville. Business is booming. They found natural gas there and you know what that means. They are not about to hold still for bank robberies." Flo was pleading now.

"They got a rifle club," I remembered. "They shoot real good, too."

That made them all laugh. The idea of townspeople shooting it out with the Daltons was too much for them to digest.

"Northfield," Flo said. "You remember what happened in Northfield? The local yokels shot the James boys and the Younger brothers all to hell."

"And they were only tryin' one bank," I added.

"They done it all wrong," said Grat. "Like Bob says, the Daltons is bigger and better than the Jameses."

Flo said, "The James boys stole thousands for your hundreds and lasted eighteen years because they were careful."

"They didn't have no woman plannin' for 'em," said Grat. "This here's Bob's plan."

"And ours," said Emmett real proud. "We all talked it over."

"Coffeyville is the place I purely hate," Bob said. His little eyes got hot. "We starved as kids in that goddam town. They treated us like dirt. We didn't have nothin', no matter how we tried. Oh, they give us charity. I can still see them old biddies with their beans and potatoes and side meat cluckin' over Mama. And purely hatin' Papa."

"Not meaning disrespect, but your mother got sick of your father in the end," said Flo. "You know it's true. He owed everybody in town."

"He died there. Sick and busted," Bob said as if that was the final argument. "Nobody give a damn."

"I remember those old women," said Emmett. "I remember how it made us feel, like niggers or worse."

"Worse is right because we ain't niggers," Bob said. "Raggedy clothes, workin' at anything we could get for a handout or a penny. Coffeyville's got to pay us for that."

Broadwell said, "It's very understandable." He had been raised in a wealthy family and he suffered for those poor Dalton kids. It didn't make sense to me. Nobody had made me any bed of roses when I was growin' up. All I knew was that I had to work and starve a little and work some more, but there was plenty more like me and we didn't think anything of it. Somehow or other we had plenty of fun. I remembered how we had played baseball in Coffeyville and all that, and it occurred to me I would have been a hell of a lot better off if I would have stayed right there. John Kloehr had been a pretty good boss, and now that the town was rich I might've amounted to somethin'.

The country was full of poor boys when I was growin' up. I had figured it out that people with no money workin' a twelve-hour day didn't have time for much fun exceptin' on the bed. So they kept havin' kids they couldn't support. It pushed the boys out on the towns, and there was too many of us so we had to work cheap. It was just the way of things, and the Daltons wasn't any different from me or anybody else.

But they thought they were different. They kept boastin' and arguin' down Flo all afternoon. She kept tellin' them the truth and they kept mockin' her because of past failures. I seen it wasn't any use and kept my mouth shut unless some one of 'em asked me a question. They yapped and yelled at Flo, specially Grat, who got drunker and drunker, and I began to think this was gettin' dangerous. I tried to get her attention and let her know somehow that she was wastin' her breath, but she kept at them—she never did give up until the bitter end. Finally she hit on a lulu of a notion.

"Bob, how many people know about this plan?"

"Just us." He thought a minute. "Well, there's brother Bill. And Doolin—he chickened out."

"You didn't try to bring in any other boys?"

"Well, a couple, maybe. Bitter Creek, he's gone. Maybe one or two others. They're all good boys; nobody'll talk."

"They all drink a lot of booze," she said, "and you know what that does to a tongue. Look at Grat."

"You shut your damn mouth," Grat yelled.

She went on at Bob. "Now does there happen to be anybody who wanted to join and you wouldn't have them?"

"Ha! Just one bum. And he's in jail."

"In jail?"

"Yeah. The dumb fool tried to hold up a post office and he got caught."

"Who caught him?"

"Why, Chris Madsen."

"And this bum is in Madsen's jail?"

"What of it?"

"You don't think Madsen didn't talk to him? Maybe offer him a deal if he'd peach on the Daltons?"

"That's crazy, Flo."

"Is it? You think Madsen's not after you tooth and nail since those two doctors got shot at Adair?"

"Nobody knows who shot them. They was wild shots got the doctors. We didn't do it."

"One is dead. And people think different about doctors than they do a Charlie Montgomery."

Bob glared at her. Montgomery was the man him and Grat killed after Bob's first girl was stolen. "You got a helluva nerve bringin' that up. That was years ago."

"It's just an example," she said. "Bob, this is a bad deal. This just won't work. I think Timothy and me had better leave."

"Oh, no you don't," howled Grat. "No way to let yawl run loose with your tongues a-waggin'."

She paid no attention to Grat. "What do you say, Bob? Timothy is against it and he's only a boy. You don't need him."

"We need him," said Grat. "He goes along. Far as that's concerned, you can ride and shoot. Make her go along, Bob."

"No, I couldn't do that," Bob said. "That ain't right. But we need Timothy."

"He's no good in a shootout."

"The way we do it there won't be no shootout. We're gonna make them people toe the line. They'll be too surprised and too scared to do any shootin'."

"So you're going to keep us here."

Bob said, "Well, look at your own argument. It's close to time, just a few days, now that we got the horses."

"Which we brought to you."

He seemed a bit uncomfortable. "All right, how did I know you were goin' to be against us?"

"Then we're prisoners?"

"Aw, don't say it like that. After all, Flo, you're my gal."

She took a few steps toward the creek. She wasn't bigger than a minute but she seemed to grow taller. She turned around and faced them all. Her voice was quiet but it had a sting like a rattlesnake.

"So that's what it's come to. I put in years trying to build something, an organization, a smart crew. I stole for you. I spied and connived and put my neck in a noose more than once. You sonofabitch, I fucked for you."

"Now, Flo." Bob squirmed.

"I let an old man paw me for months just to get money for your booze and your whores. I lied and wore myself out and took chances. I broke my ass in a saddle. If there is anything I haven't done for you, Bob Dalton, you might name it."

He said, "You done your best, Flo."

"Yes. I did my best. Now you want to go and get killed. Well, the hell with you. I'm finished."

"It's the biggest thing I ever thought up in my life," he said, and you could see the stubbornness in him. "Ain't nobody goin' to stop me from doin' it."

She said, "Timothy, saddle up our horses."

"No," said. Grat. He had that gun out. He was always yankin' it and flourishin' it. "I won't hold for that."

Bob said, "He's right. You can camp with us, Flo. And you can go when we make our start. Timothy, he goes along."

She sort of slumped. She sat down on a log and put her face in her hands. Grat just laughed, but Bob was unhappy and the others pretended it wasn't happening, looking everywhere but at Flo. I went over and sat beside her and put my arm around her.

She leaned against me and whispered, "We'll get away. Play mouse for them."

So we played like we were licked. Emmett cooked like always, and we scarcely ate the food and mooned around. There was no escapin' Grat—drunk or sober, the bastard kept his eye on us. But we could whisper together when she pretended to cry on my shoulder.

"They're crazy as bedbugs," I said.

"You can't ride in with them."

"I just want to get you loose. I'll find some way to escape."

"Timothy?"

"Yes?"

"If I do get away—I'll be at Woodward."

"You'll make it. Wait and see."

They separated us at night. I lay with my head on the

bedroll and thought it out. They could make me ride with them, no question. Too many of them were watchin' and too many guns had no conscience about shootin' a fifteen-year-old boy who didn't agree with Bob. But if the Daltons were smarter than me, then I deserved whatever I got, that was for sure. I only wanted to get Flo far enough away so she wouldn't be mixed up in it. That was the problem.

I saw Bob go over to where she lay wrapped in her blankets. He whispered at her, trying to make up, to get her to go into the woods with him, figurin' anything could be worked out by him layin' her. He had that kind of a mind. He worked at it for a while, then he give up. I heard her last line.

"The only way you'll ever get to me is to have your brave boys stretch me out while you rape me. That's final."

He went back to his own blankets. It took a while to get asleep, and I didn't have any real plan, neither.

It was the 4th of October. They had watched us day and night. They had never said a word in our hearing about their plans but we knew they were going to move out. I had given up the idea of getting Flo away under cover of darkness—that's when they expected us to make a break. I had also given up on getting away myself. There was just one thing in my mind—to help Flo go free.

The thing was, I had to get a saddle on her horse and this was truly impossible in a small encampment like they had. So I had to wait, and she waited with me and she got thinner by the hour, I thought. She was haunted by the whole mess, the plans of Bob and our own danger. But she still had a sharp eye out, she still knew how to signal me in ways they couldn't see or understand. You got to remember, these were no brainy gents, these were really dumb outlaws.

But there is a very big trouble dealin' with such dummies. They don't react to surprises or anything. They just go their way, and this bunch had a way of shootin'. Although I knew Flo had the guts and I knew I was ready to do anything to help her, we had to realize both of us could be dead before there was any raid on Coffeyville.

I was taking care of the horses like always. That morning I took 'em down to water and Grat was watchin' me. It was just about daylight and everybody else was sleepin'. Grat had been at the jug of alcohol but seemed far enough awake to keep me from saddlin' the pony Flo had ridden to camp.

My sorrel had been with me a long time and we knew each other real well, the way it is with man and any beast he owns. He was a high-spirited horse, although used to me, and always good humored if I treated him like he expected. I got him upstream from the others. He lowered his head to drink.

I got between Flo's pony and Grat and leaned down and took the sorrel's ear between my teeth and clamped down hard. He reared up and kicked and I hit him on the flank. He must have been completely scared out of his wits at such goin's on. I grabbed the halter on Flo's pony and the sorrel rammed into the horse next to him and started a stampede downstream.

I yelled, "Grat! Head 'em off!"

Like I say, Grat wasn't too smart ever, and when drinking he was real stupid. He began runnin' after the cavvy. I snatched up Flo's saddle and had it on the pony in what had to be world's record time. She came with her bedroll and I slung that up and she went with it.

Now the camp was awake. I fell down and rolled into the water, hollerin' with my mouth full of water. Flo drove in the spurs she had worn to bed the night before, just on a chance this silly plan worked. She went west and she bent low against a bullet and the pony flew like the wind, well rested and ready to go.

Nobody fired a shot. Grat was chasin' the horses and Bob couldn't shoot his own ex-gal no matter if he wanted. We had figured it out he was always readin' the papers and boastin' about his stories and some had made him out a sort of Robin Hood and so forth and he didn't dare. They all was millin' around and Grat was yelpin' and I got out of the creek and ran to help Grat.

We got the horses easy—they really didn't want to stampede—and I talked in the ear of the sorrel and eased him back to camp. Most of them were more worried the horses might get away than about Flo anyway, but Bob grabbed me and slammed me against a tree. He had to take it out on somebody.

I stammered at him. "I dunno what happened . . . The sorrel broke and then there was Flo . . . You know how she is, always so fast and all . . . I fell into the creek . . . I just dunno."

Grat said, "I'll saddle up and git her. I'll finish her."

I thought the others agreed with him, but Bob shook his head. "We're ridin' today. We don't need to worry about her squealin', we all know that. Maybe it's just as well. I couldn't figure what to do with her anyway, how she is and all."

"I agree," said Broadwell. "We have enough on our minds. And we should start today. It's bad luck to change plans."

"Damn bad," said Bob. "We're all set. We got everything lined up."

He turned me loose. I went to the horses and they all began saddling up. I kept apart as much as I could, tryin' not to be noticed. Grat growled at me but he didn't suspicion anything really; he was just like that, and he put me together with Flo and hated us both.

Well, we rode up the Verdigris River toward Kansas on a very appropriate trace known as Whiskey Trail. If ever anybody rode a whiskey trail always and forever it was the Daltons. I knew it well—it led to Coffeyville. They had not told me a word about the plan and I didn't ask any questions.

They were in high spirits. They had saved one of the good bottles Flo had brought for this occasion. They passed it back and forth and talked. Their voices were kinda sharp and strained, but it was always that way when they rode—I reckon everyone who ever went into danger was alike. I was the only glum rider, bringin' up in the rear. Bob and Grat led, then Emmett and Broadwell and the silent Powers. It was a nice October day, if you was just out for a canter in the sunshine.

A whole bunch of Coffeyville names kept runnin' through my head, people I had known when I was there. John Kloehr; Charlie Grump, the drayman; Lucius Baldwin, the Methodist store clerk; George Cubine and Charlie Brown, the shoemakers; Tom Babb, who worked part time in the bank—the First National—Henry Isham of the hardware store—they wouldn't stop walkin' through my mind. Carey Seaman the barber, Dr. Wells, Al Reynolds, the mild old Marshal Charlie Connelly—what would they be doing when the Daltons came in? Every one of them knew the brothers by sight. Broadwell and Powers was strangers, but the Daltons were like home folk, not well liked nor respected but still familiar to the people of the town.

I got jolted out of it when Emmett dragged Bob back to the rear of the parade and began talking so I could hear.

"I don't like Grat going into the First National with Dick and Bill. You know how he is. Why don't you let me take it and you go into the Condon with Grat?"

"You heard what we said about changin' plans." But Bob's voice was soft and easy. "I want you with me. You're the baby and I want you where I can take care."

"But Grat—he can't lead and he never did rob a bank before."

"Neither did we. But we got it figured, haven't we?"

"Oh, sure, Bob. We got Jesse beat at last. I know that. I just thought I could do it better than Grat."

"Maybe you could. But there'll be three of them. Dick and Bill are good fighters. Dick's pretty smart."

"I don't like it, Bob."

"You go 'long, now. We're goin' to do this my way."

Emmett rode on up and Bob gave me a hard look. He said, "When we camp tonight you'll know what you're to do. And you better do it, boy."

"I'm here, ain't I?"

"You better be there, where I want you."

"Okay, Bob."

We rode awhile, then he said, "Kid, I'm sorry about Flo. She was a good old gal."

"She done plenty for us."

"Like she said. She sure showed spunk, tellin' me off like she did."

"She's got plenty of spunk."

"Spunk and guts," he said. "I'll get together with her

when this here is over and we got the loot. Where you think she went?"

"Gosh, Bob, how should I know? She's got plenty places to hide out, all over the country."

"That's right. But she can't hide from me. I got ways of findin' people." He canted his eyes at me. "Don't you forget that neither, Timothy."

"Why should I worry about it?"

"Just so you do your job tomorrow."

"Long as it ain't shootin' anybody."

"You may have to do that, too."

"Well, you know how I am."

"You might have to get over it."

I said, "Well then, if you say so, maybe I do. You're the boss."

He liked that, bein' called the boss. He rode up front again. I thought I knew now what he wanted of me. I was to mind the horses and shoot a rifle to keep people under cover. That was an old James Boys trick—everybody knew about it, the papers and the dime novels and the magazines were all full of it, the way bank robbers did. If that's all he knew, what he had read about it, I thought, we sure were in for trouble.

We came across the Kansas line and then we were in country familiar to the Daltons and me, farm after farm stretching all the way to Coffeyville. When we reached the Davis place it was late afternoon, and this was where Bob had decided to spend the night. There was a stream and some dense thicket, and Mr. Davis never did see us or have any notion we was thereabouts.

Bob directed us to loosen the cinches but leave the saddles on and to tie each horse to a tree and be ready for anything at a minute's notice. He wasn't nervous, he was just edgy, gettin' so close to all that loot. He sent Grat and Emmett over to a neighborin' cornfield owned by Widow J. F. Savage for corn to feed the horses. We had our own cold vittles, and we sat around and Bob talked. He had to tell me the plans now, and he wanted to go over them once more anyway so that everybody would have them down cold turkey.

He took a sharp stick and drew a rough map of Coffeyville in the dirt. It was accurate enough—he had been there for the booze lately and the memory was good. He put the two banks across from each other. He lined out the alley around the corner from the First National and looked at me.

"There's where we leave the horses. We do this afoot so as to take 'em by surprise. You'll be right there. You'll have your rifle. If a ruckus starts you'll shoot."

"Okay, Bob." There was no use argufyin'—I didn't have a chance to make a point. It was all set in his head. I seen that the alley was a bad idea even then. The horses should be nearer to the banks, maybe right in the center of Union Street.

He squatted there talkin' like an idiot and I got a detached feeling of a sudden like you sometimes do—like I wasn't a part of it. I was removed, lookin' at them from the outside, from far away but seein' them clear, maybe for the first time. There they were, five rumpled young fellas settin' around talkin' about robbin' two banks at once in a busy town that knew three of them like a book, had known them since they were buttons.

They didn't look like robbers. The nice clothes they had got from Flo were dark-coats and pants and regular ridin' boots like everyone wore, nothin' fancy. Their hats was just—hats. If it wasn't for the guns—they carried plenty guns—nobody would take them for anything but ordinary riders.

But they had stole and they had killed. They had killed at Wharton and before that. They had fired shots which were heard around the country through telegraph and newspapers and all. The oldest of them was thirty and one. The youngest was twenty years of age. They had never known anything that suited them exceptin' when drunk on the miserable proceeds of their robbin'. And maybe in bed with Flo and others, although there was nothin' much to their beddin' down, as Flo had told me. They were closer to animals in that way.

Now here they were talkin' this nonsense, and there was Timothy Bradford Younger listenin' to them and knowin' they were lookin' for bad trouble in the most stupid fashion. It was this moment when I separated from them.

I could not just walk on, you know. I could not ride out with a fond farewell like in the songs. There wasn't any music to this whatsoever, no romantic ballad of the wild ridin' men of the road. It wasn't like that. It was honky mean, dirty, lowdown dumbness in a country that was gettin' ready to defend itself against the Ozark people, who all stemmed from William Clarke Quantrill, the Bloody Bastard.

It was for me also the first time I wasn't under the direct influence of Flo Quick. She was not part of this, I had no instructions from her. This forced me to think on my own, and I thought about Coffeyville and my time there and what this gang was planning and what it could mean to the people I had known there. Not that they were such great and noble people, but they were great at mindin' their own business and had long since give up shootin' and killin' on the main streets and all that. They were the new world, with businesses and all that, people tryin' to make it through life by hard work and savin's in the banks which the Daltons were plannin' to rob. It was a kind of colored postcard in my mind, the way the town was and the way we were out here campin' for the night.

It wasn't any divine vision, just a plain postcard made from a photograph which told me where I stood and what could happen to me. It wasn't any crossroad between right and wrong—I didn't think about right nor wrong, only about what could happen to me and them and the town. Mainly me, because I was now different and apart from them—that was most clear, the clearest thing of all. It wasn't noble nor nothin', it was self preservation—how did I get out of it with a whole skin, without them or some damn fool townsman shootin' me in the ass?

Bob was lookin' at me, waitin' for an answer to somethin' I never did hear and I said, "Sure, Bob. Whatever you figure is right."

"You just spray 'em with lead," he said. "I don't give a damn about how you feel now, Timothy. This here is the time to be a man. Them people treated us and our papa dirt mean and rotten. If they start anything, you shoot, and not over their heads, neither, you believe me."

"Sure, Bob. This is the time." I would tell him anything he wanted to hear. I wasn't part of it anymore.

"Maybe a hundred thousand in them two banks," he said. "This time we see Jesse and raise him outa the pot."

Emmett said, "That's right, we beat Jesse this time."

Those two, they couldn't think of anything else. Grat, he

was too thick to worry about the James Boys or anything else, and Broadwell was too smart and Powers was like a nothin', the least of them all. I had never thought them smart, and now I knew how really down dumb they were.

Bob said, "Remember, Timothy, you are a Younger."

"Yessir." And where were the Youngers?

"Any Younger can whip any ten Coffeyvillers."

"I reckon."

So they went on and on and I thought they would never go to sleep. They wasn't scared, they was high. Only Grat needed the booze; the others was high on tomorrow and the money they would steal and the stories that would be in all the papers about the Great Dalton Gang.

No, they wasn't scared. A reptile hasn't got much brains, but you wouldn't play around with moccasins nor rattlers. And they would kill as quick as any snake.

Then Bob got very dramatical. They had this little fire in the canebreak—not enough to attract attention but a sturdy little flame—and he took out some bits of paper and a letter and stuff.

He said, "Boys, just in case somethin' goes wrong— which it can't, but anyways—we wouldn't want our families to know who we are or anything. Right? So let's burn anything we got on us which would give us away."

Emmett said, "Bob's right. Our dear mama mustn't ever know. I got this picture of Julia—she mustn't know."

Now can you beat that? Here's three brothers ridin' into a town where everybody and his cousin knows 'em, and they are goin' to hide who they are if something goes wrong, which would mean they are dead or captured? Can you believe it? But that's what they did, all solemn, even

143

Broadwell, whose family lived in Hutchinson, Kansas, and was rich and as well known as any Dalton.

I rolled up in my blankets. I didn't have anything to give me away and if I did it wouldn't get me in trouble if I used the brains God gave me, is the way I felt about it. I don't know how long they sat and talked and talked. I turned them off and went into my own head and did a lot of thinkin' away from them. It ain't easy for a fifteen year old to see himself dead, but I done it. And I knew that if I didn't use my brains it could happen.

I tried to think what Flo would do and remembered somethin' she had said: "The simplest way is mostly the best way."

Well, I couldn't come up with any clever plan so I figured to do what came naturally, the simplest way. And if it came down to it, I decided one thing: Better to be shot and killed by the Daltons than by somebody in Coffeyville. I don't know why, but right then, the way I felt, that seemed to be true.

The last I heard was Bob and Emmett talkin' both at once about Jesse James and how they were going to put him in the shade. Then I must've fell asleep.

The morning came, grey and early. They looked worse now, unshaven and bleary-eyed, Grat grumblin' because Bob wouldn't let him have more than an eye-opener from the jug. They cinched up and Bob called them together again. He had a paper sack. He began to take stuff from it and I couldn't believe my own eyes.

He had beards and mustaches and funny noses and all that kinda junk kids wore on Halloween. He truly did. He began handin' it out to Grat and Emmett and me.

He said, "Nobody knows Dick or Bill. But they might recognize us too soon, y' see. So we'll wear these here disguises."

Grat put on a beard, and I tell you he looked weird. Bob wore a mustache and the funny nose, but the nose bothered him and he took it off. Emmett wore sideburns and a small beard. Bob gave me somethin' about the same but I put it in my pocket.

He said, "You better wear somethin', boy. They know you in Coffeyville."

"Sure, Bob, later. It tickles me right now." I had a linsey-woolsey hat which had a droopy brim, and had put away my good hat in the bedroll. I sure didn't want to be knowed by anybody who might see us, but a beard on a fifteen-year-old boy would draw as much attention as an elephant walkin' down Eighth Street with a beer in one hand and a pretzel in the other, I figured. And the way the Daltons looked it wouldn't be any different for them.

That's the way it started on the 5th of October, 18 and 92, when the Daltons began their ride to Coffeyville. That was the great brain of Bob workin' as usual, like a dim lantern on a stormy night. I swear to ginney, I was never so scared in my life to be with this crowd on this day.

We came across Onion Creek and onto the Davis field. There were a couple cows grazin', and damned if, when we took down a rail to ride off onto the county road, Emmett didn't replace the rails so the cows wouldn't stray. It's real funny the things men'll do sometimes.

It was so early and we so close to town that we rode very slow, which made it worse and also maybe better for me. I mean, it was nerve-wrackin' to go so snail-like but it gave me time to think. Only I didn't seem to have any thoughts that was goin' to help. Truth to tell, I was paralyzed from the neck up, listenin' to Bob go over the plans again—that alley for the horses, the two banks with Grat takin' charge of the robbery of the Condon, how they would ride out easy with the town all cowed down and scared to stick out a head to see what was happening.

Then I seen this gal ridin' a pony. One look and I knew who she was. I yanked my wool hat down and slumped in the saddle. I had fallen back behind the others; now I moved in among 'em. They didn't look behind them. I don't know what they would've done if they had seen her.

She was Jenny Brown, and I knew her and her folks. She was a year younger'n me and somewhat blossomed since she was twelve—a fat girl, ugly. She was ridin' west like we was. I never did like Jenny but I hoped to hell she wouldn't recognize me or catch up or anything. I didn't want to see even a fat ugly gal layin' in a ditch.

Just as I was about chokin' Jenny turned off on a side road. The Dalton gang still hadn't seen her. She could have been three men with guns, but they were too busy makin' their plans and spendin' the money they hadn't got to look behind them.

We niggled along and came to the farm where the Daltons had lived when they were young ones. It was a beat up place at best, a tenant farm which Lewis Dalton, their dear papa, hadn't bothered to farm. Bob began to run down the Coffeyville people again. Emmett had a sob story about his mama and his poor unfortunate papa— who was the deadbeat of two States and a Territory.

Broadwell and Powers believed it all, but I knew better and it just served to drive me even further away from the Dalton brothers. They had the big mouth and the sad story whenever it suited them. Other times there just wasn't nobody like the Daltons—they were the greatest people and best family in the United States.

Finally the sun got higher and we come to the cheese factory, which was close to the town. My head ached and it was like my brain would bust out of my skull, but I still didn't have the slightest notion how to get away and out of the mess I was into.

The next scarey thing to me was a buggy comin' toward us, from Coffeyville. There were two people in it. I dropped back again and was ready to turn into a ditch but Bob snapped at me to keep up. I strained to see who it might be. It was Mr. and Mrs. R. H. Hollingsworth of the Methodist Church where Lucius Baldwin attended, and they knew me—they were drivin' one of Kloehr's rigs. As they came close I hung down over the neck of the sorrel on the opposite side from them. They looked awful close at the Daltons with those crazy beards, but they drove on to the west. They didn't see me, I knew that.

I got my breath and began dropping further back. Bob had his eyes ahead now, with Coffeyville in view. The town was busy, as it always was early in the morning. The banks opened at eight and it was gettin' on to that time and Bob figured not to be either too early or too late. We were to the edge of town when a carriage drove out. I saw the Seldomridge brothers—goin' out to collect from some of their tenants, I reckoned—rich men, kind of like misers. They also took a hard look at the gang, and with the sun bright it seemed they could not miss those false beards and mustaches. But they were men that minded their own considerable business. They just rode on.

And as they did my mind came out of the daze. It was like Flo had said, make it simple and make it fast. Being at the tag end of the bunch, I let the Seldomridge rig go past me. For a minute I was out of sight, blocked by the horses and carriage. The Seldomridges got a look at me— but I was ridin' away from the Daltons on the sorrel. I was going at right angles, around the town and away from Eighth Street, which was where the road led to. I was going fast and the brothers in the carriage was lookin' after me. The gang didn't dare shoot. If they did, they would have to kill the Seldomridges, too, and while this might have been all right with them, it wasn't the time for it. I took a cut at the far end of the street as though I was going west away from town because I wanted to give them the idea that I was runnin' away, scared because Bob had said I had to shoot people and all. I knew the way his mind worked and that he would believe this.

In fact, do not believe that I didn't strongly think myself of going on, all the way, fast as the sorrel could take me. I thought of Flo at Woodward and how she would be waiting for the news and how I could get to her with my money belt. And maybe we could get clean away to some new place. Then I realized that I was thinkin' about Flo like she was my mother, which was pretty strange. It was runnin' home to mother no matter how I looked at it.

So I swung the sorrel around when I was out of sight of the Dalton gang. I knew where the Daltons was going to leave their horses in the alley off Eighth Street, so I made a full circle and came fast in on Ninth Street. I headed for Kloehr's livery stable, because that had been my place. But I didn't know what I was going to do when I got there.

I had taken myself away from the Daltons, that was for sure. Partin' from them forever, that was one thing. Rousin' the town and yellin' that they was comin' to rob the banks, that was another thing altogether. I had rode with them, I had held their horses, and most of all, Flo Quick had been my only best friend. I couldn't get around it. I slowed down the sorrel, thinkin' about it. I didn't stop headin' for Kloehr's, but again my mind was in a tangle. Even a grownup would've had to stop and ponder on it, I still believe. It wasn't any one-two-three question of what to do and how to behave.

It was also a question of bein' a squealer. Any kind of a tattletale was hated in the country. We was brought up not to tell on people. It was a hell of a lot more to us than religion. Maybe it was part of what little religion there was in us, any of us. It went strict against the grain, and even the people that anyone might tattle to would not have respect for a person, and that was the way it was, and still is for the most part, if you look into it.

So the upshot of it was, I sneaked into Kloehr's by the back way, leadin' my horse. I still didn't know what to do. I was standin' first on one foot and then the other like a boy by a heap of manure when I heard voices. It was Kloehr and someone else.

Kloehr said, "I tell you I got word from Madsen again. The Daltons are comin' this way sooner or later. A jailbird sung in Madsen's ear, one of them that wanted to join up and Bob wouldn't let him."

The other man said, "They wouldn't hit this town where

they are known. Not in daylight. They ain't that dumb."

Kloehr said, "Isham's got rifles stacked. The rifle club is ready. Everybody's ready but that Marshal we got."

"Charlie don't look for no trouble."

"He should be a schoolteacher, not a lawman."

"I dunno, maybe he's right. I don't want no part of fightin' the Daltons. They come here, they won't get any trouble from me."

"Yahhh," said Kloehr. "Too many like you."

"I suppose you'd shoot 'em down?"

"Like dogs," said Kloehr. "That's what they are, dogs. I'd kill 'em all with one bullet if I could."

So that was enough for me. I tippy-toed away and went down Ninth Street and tied up the sorrel. Then I walked back, turnin' up my wool hat so that I might look like a country boy comin' home if anybody recognized me, or just a plain farmhand if they didn't. I put my gun in the bedroll and stuffed the revolver under my jacket, which was loose enough to hide the bulge . . . just in case. Then I looked for a high place.

The only place I could get atop of was Isham's Hardware Store, which had a back stairway almost to the roof. I remembered it and ran up the stairs and crawled out to where I could see up and down Union Street. The Condon Bank was directly opposite and the First National Bank was next door to Isham's, between it and the Rammel Brothers Drug Store. The two banks faced each other, like was said before. I could also see the alley to the west, where Bob had said to leave the horses with me and me to shoot anybody who started anything. I climbed up high on the false front and perched there, and that's where I was during it, the

Dalton raid on Coffeyville, and that's how I saw it all.

Now this part I am going to have to tell the way I saw it plus the way I know it happened where I did not see it. There were plenty of people telling all kinds of tales, and the newspaper, the *Journal*, had it pretty straight, and the fella that wrote the book, he got it from the newspaper, but there were some things came out later which were correct. The thing that I thought about, up high there above it all, was that the Daltons were bad enough but if the town was warned and knew they were comin' and were more or less organized and ready, why didn't they just let the Daltons have the loot and then waylay them out of town and not get innocent bystanders and others all shot to hell? The other thing I thought is that there ain't no damn heroes. Show me a hero and I'll show you a sick person or a dumb one or one who is a hero by accident. Kloehr was no hero—he was a town man anxious to show off his skill with a rifle, and that's not any better than the Daltons was. That's why I didn't squeal to Kloehr—because I wasn't any hero neither, and I didn't like what Kloehr said nor the way he said he would shoot them down like dogs. I figured, let's see him go against the Gang, and let the best ones win.

Of course, I didn't have any idea what would happen. Had I known, I still ain't sure what I'd have done. I ain't at all sure.

There I was away high up, flattened out so nobody could spot me without lookin' straight at me, cranin' to see what was happening on Union Street. Kloehr's was now west of me, behind Slossen's Drug Store. There seemed to be more people in the streets than I had seen before. The town was busier and bigger. Cyrus Lee's ice wagon was in front of the First National Bank almost, drippin' water, remindin' me of the times Cyrus had chipped me off a chunk for suckin' on when the weather was Kansas hot. There wasn't time to do more than take a quick look, because they were comin' out through the alley where they had left the horses. They were trottin' along carryin' their rifles and still wearin' those damfool disguises.

The strange part was that they got as far as they did before bein' recognized. Some kids hollered at them but they paid no attention. They were going pretty good toward the two banks, Bob and Emmett toward the First National and Grat leadin' Broadwell and Powers toward the Condon Bank.

Then they came to Alex McKenna's store and were passing it when Alex took a hard look. He knew them, all three of the Daltons. He saw the rifles and the way they were trottin' and sort of crouchin' and lookin' right and left, and he yelled.

"It's them damn Daltons! Hey, it's the Dalton bunch!"

That's when Kloehr and a couple of the others of the rifle club came to hear of it. I didn't see them hustlin' to get in on anything, but they did go for their guns.

McKenna ran into Isham's Hardware, and so did Cyrus Lee. No doubt about it, there was some information given out and they had talked it over, what they would do IF the Daltons came and how they would do it, because others ran for Isham's, where the guns and ammunition were stacked. And some ran for the boondocks, you can bet on that. I seen 'em go. They heard "the Daltons" and they took off, and I could name them but won't because they are out of my story and the hell with them.

Matter of fact, after McKenna called their names there was plenty of time for any sort of action. But Bob and Emmett got into the First National and the others into the Condon and not a soul tried to prevent them. It was some time before anybody did anything but mill around with rifles in their hands and grab up ammunition and talk loud and fast, so nobody could understand anybody. Joe Kloehr wasn't any place in sight, not then.

Now is where I got to depend on what was written and told and all that, plus what I know about the Daltons, because I wasn't in the banks and couldn't hear what went on. It's nothin' new much. People tend to get a bit mixed up and several told it different ways and all, but it's about what must've happened, all considered.

There were three men in the First National when Bob and Emmett crashed in all guns and keyed up and hollerin' that it was a holdup and makin' 'em put up their hands. Tom Ayres, the cashier, was behind the counter, and the teller, man name of Shepherd, was sittin' at a desk near the vault.

Old Bob says to Ayres, "I want all the money in this bank, Tom."

Now here was Bob in whiskers and all, who had destroyed all the evidence of who they were so nobody would identify them—here he was calling Ayres by his first name. That was the Dalton way always—find some way of screwing things up.

At that, things went good in the First National. Emmett found Bert Ayres in the back and stood him up with the others. Tom Ayres wasn't takin' chances with rifles down his throat—he began pushing out money. Then Emmett saw the vault was open and he went in there and grabbed up everything in sight and put it in the wheat sack.

Somebody looked in the window to see what was going on and Emmett spotted them. He bellowed at 'em and a man named Boothby came in scared to pieces, hands up. There was a kid out there, Jack Long, only about ten. Emmett motioned at him and Jack beat it up the street yellin' his lungs out that the Daltons were robbin' the First National, as if everybody in Coffeyville didn't know that by now. Thing was, Emmett was a big talker but he couldn't kill in cold blood. He was never like that.

The Ayreses, father and son, moved as slow as possible, but Bob and Emmett had time. There were men with guns now—I could see them—but they were in groups and it reminded you of the old mouse story of "Who's goin' to bell the cat?" You get a bunch together and you have to have a leader, otherwise they will yap a lot and do nothin'. There was plenty of 'em that day who waved guns but didn't use 'em.

When Bob and Emmett had got all the loot they thought they could manage—and it was enough, around twenty thousand—they started out the door with the seven men ahead of them, the bank people and the others, includin' Boothby. Their idea was to use the citizens as a shield and to join up with Grat and Dick and Bill and get to the horses and ride out. It wasn't the worst idea in the world, at that, but there was no sign of Grat. Further and more, George Cubine, the shoemaker, and C. S. Cox, a member of the rifle club, had got into the drug store across the street and began shooting. Cubine had a Winchester and Cox a revolver. They didn't hit anybody but they started the whole damn war, and whatever anybody else did that day, it was them two that got it off the ground and into action.

It was a strange feelin', being up where I was above it all, knowing the boys, having been with them all those months off and on, through the robberies, and now watchin' people shoot at 'em. It was like watching something that you ought to be in but at the same time you are damn glad you are not in it. After the first minute or so it didn't seem real. That is, it didn't until the blood began to run—then it was too real.

After Cubine and Cox started it there began to be a real storm. People were shooting so often from so many angles it was a wonder the town wasn't wiped out. Bob and Emmett sure couldn't cross the square, even with their screen of seven hostages. So they sensibly enough went out the back door of the bank, leavin' the captives behind. They had a chance to make it north in the alley to the firehouse, then west where nobody was lookin' for them, and then south to the other alley, where they had left their horses and where I could see a clear way for them out of town. It really looked right then as if they were getting away with it all.

But then there was old Grat still in the Condon Bank with the other two boys, and we have to go back and tell what happened in there, near as can be made out. It wasn't smooth and easy like the First National. If it had been and Coffeyville had been real organized and used good sense, there would have been less blood and guts to the story.

Emmett had been right—Bob never should've put Grat in charge of the raid on the Condon Bank. Maybe it was because Grat was the oldest and the meanest of them, maybe because Bob wanted Emmett the kid where he could watch over him—nobody knows, but he stuck to his decision. Truthfully, neither Broadwell nor Powers was much shakes as a leader, and then there was the belief among the Daltons that they were the biggest muckity-mucks in the robbery business. It probably couldn't have been any other way.

Grat and the boys got into the bank all right. First thing anybody knew there they were, and once again, Grat was recognized behind his false whiskers. Tom Babb was working in the Condon that day, and he'd known the Daltons all his life. He saw the masks on Dick and Bill and the guns and all and he ducked. He didn't say a word, didn't warn anybody, he just run and hid. Which proved Tom had good sense, because Grat might've shot him dead if he peeped.

One of the bank's co-owners, Carpenter, was in the bank, and when Grat yelled for them to put up their hands and count out the loot, he didn't hesitate. He also knew Grat, and he didn't think the other two were Daltons but he didn't want to buck loaded rifles, neither. There was two doors to the Condon and Dick guarded one and Bill the other while Grat collected the money. This was good sense, but there was big old Grat and there was one cool head, a stubborn and brainy sort of fellow name of Charlie Ball, and he was the cashier. He came out of his office in the back to see what was goin' on and walked right into Grat's rifle muzzle. Charlie didn't blink. He'd been warned about the Daltons along with everybody else and he had thought a lot about them and what could be done if they hit the Condon.

Carpenter evidently hadn't thought or hadn't believed, because he was scared stiff. Grat kept telling Ball to fill the wheat sack and Ball began sticking silver dollars into it.

"Never mind the goddam silver, I want gold and bank notes," Grat yelled. "What's in that goddam vault there? Get it the hell open."

"Can't do it, Grat," said Ball.

"The hell you can't. Then let him do it."

Carpenter just stood there and shook.

Ball said, "It's got a set-lock."

"What in tarnation is that?"

Broadwell called over, "That means it won't open until a certain time, Grat."

"What the hell time?" Now Grat was shook and Carpenter was scared and Powers, looking out the door, put in his two cents worth.

"Hey, there's people out there with guns."

"The hell with them chickenshits," Grat said. "What time does that damn thing open?"

"Nine-thirty," said Ball.

"What the hell time is it now?"

"Twenty minutes past," said Ball, looking at his watch but not showing it to Grat. It was past nine-thirty and there wasn't any time lock on the vault, but Ball knew his Grat and was willing to take a chance, and of all the people in Coffeyville that day he was the smartest. Only thing, in his way he also contributed to what happened. Even he didn't think to just hand them the money and set a trap planned in advance to get them as they rode out. People always did set a great store by hard cash and always will. Won't trust it out of their hands for twenty seconds.

So there was Grat foolin' around with silver dollars and some cash Ball doled out to him and figuring he had ten minutes to glory. If he had just busted the vault, which was more of a chest-like thing, he could have taken the loot and joined Bob and Emmett for what chance they had, which was good, since the Coffeyville people had not been so smart.

And then shooting began.

Cubine had started it and Isham was handing out guns and ammunition, and now men were getting into safe places and just firing into the banks. Two customers entered the Condon and were caught between two fires. They ducked and laid low and were safe enough. Dick and Bill began shooting back as the windows splintered. I could see this action from atop the roof. There was as much lead poppin' in Coffeyville as there had been at Bull Run. At first nobody was hit and it was just a Fourth of July sort of thing.

Then Parker Williams, squattin' on the awning of the Boswell Hardware Store across from the Condon and bangin' away with a .45 must've got lucky, because I heard Dick Broadwell holler in pain and yell at Grat:

"I'm hit in the arm. I can't use the arm."

Grat started looking for a back way out of there, forgetting about the vault and the money and everything else. There was too much hot lead coming through the front of the bank. Ball conned him again, said there wasn't any rear exit. Old Grat was consistent to the end. He emptied the wheat sack and divided the money, all but the coins. It came to a lousy thousand dollars, but Grat never did count too good—it was cash and would buy booze.

There was a back way out, as I well knew. But Grat didn't bother to look. He had a single-track mind, and the way he came in seemed the only way out and he took it. He got Broadwell on his feet and yelped at Powers.

"They can't get us. The hell with 'em. Bob'll be with us. C'mon, let's go."

And damned if they didn't. They busted right through the front door, the three of them. Dick was already bleedin', his arm hangin' loose, tryin' to work the rifle with his one good hand. Grat and Powers crouched low, as though that would help them duck lead. Everybody in Coffeyville was at it now, like in a shootin' gallery. It was an army against three men who didn't know too much what to do under the circumstances. I stared down and couldn't hardly believe what I saw. It was plain murder whichever way you looked at it, whatever side you was on, and I wasn't on either side for that time.

People shootin' at one another are always in a hurry, unless they are both very good shots and very cold-blooded. There was lead enough going back and forth as Grat and Dick and Bill emptied their rifles and the town people kept reloading and firing. There were moments when it looked like the boys would get across the square.

Then it looked from where I was as if somebody was dustin' their coats. Broadwell got another one in the back and dove off and out of sight toward the lumber yard. He was through right then so far as fight was concerned. Then Powers got it. He was the little guy and they kept pumping it to him, and he wasn't going anywhere—he just lay there and died.

Grat bled the most. They got him good. They were yellin' and whoopin' and cheerin' when he went down. The blood was awful, soaking up in the dust. He lost his false whiskers and choked and there was more blood. He tried to keep goin' and make a stand. He finally made it to a little alley off Walnut Street, where he leaned against a barn and held onto his guns and waited for help. You knew he was lookin' for Bob and Emmett by the way he kept turnin' his head, blood pourin' out of him, then fumblin' with the guns to reload, then lookin' again. He was big, and although he had always been a boozer he still had a lot of stamina. He was like a wounded bull—he just wouldn't quit. Grat had his own kind of sand. He was no coward.

Then there was confusion back of First National. When I hitched around to look, the vomit was comin' up in my throat to see what had happened to the others. Bob had come upon Lucius Baldwin. The kid didn't have any right to be there, holdin' a little pistol. He wasn't that kind—he was a church goer and a peacemaker, one of the nice boys in the town. He shoulda been like Tom Babb and knowed it wasn't his war. It was for other kind of people. But there he was with his little gun and there was Bob and Emmett, and Lucius didn't have it in him to fire a shot.

So Bob killed him without knowin' it wasn't necessary. It was the worst thing that happened that day. Killin' that young fella was a clean waste. He would never have shot Bob nor anybody else. It was a dumb damn thing.

Out on the street Gump the drayman was down, I seen then. He must've got it from one of the stray bullets. Nobody will ever know from which gun—maybe from one of the boys, maybe from one of the wild-shootin' townsfolk, whatever. He was holdin' his hand, which was all bloodied and shattered, and makin' for cover. He'd been carryin' a shotgun, which was knocked to bits by the bullet that hit him. They all wanted to kill somebody, and those that got it themselves—what can you say, they were heroes or somethin'? Not in my book. They were a bunch of dummies.

The two-by-fours and furrin' lath I was stretched on was cutting into me, but I didn't know it. There is an awful fascination to a battle you are watchin' and not into. You

160

want to yell out and tell people to do this or do that, you don't want to see people hurt and maimed and killed. But you can't stop lookin' and you know you can't do a damn thing about it, and this is the kind of nasty feeling you get, like you're apart and above it all. It ain't a good feelin' when you examine it later.

Now Bob and Emmett had to know something had gone wrong at the Condon Bank, and probably Bob was not too surprised, because in his heart he knew Grat was without brains. Anyway, they got to Union Street and fired a few shots and someone yelled at them from a grocery store and they chased him indoors. Most of the armed town people were concentratin' on poor Powers and Grat and didn't notice them at first.

George Cubine was still at Rammel's drugstore with his rifle. Bob saw he was armed and shot him and Emmett fired at him also, and down went the shoemaker. I could see he wasn't goin' to get up—there is a way they fall that tells you they are bad hit.

Then Brown did another real dumb thing. He ran out and grabbed Cubine's gun and looked for a target. Of course Bob and Emmett cleaned him, too, knocking the old man back on his ass with a volley. This was all part of the senseless things that went on, because Brown was so near-sighted he couldn't hit a bull in the butt with a shovel.

Tom Ayres had picked up a gun, too. He was maybe a hundred yards away from Bob and Emmett. By this time Bob must've had the blood lust. For no reason at all he took a shot at the cashier and hit him in the face. The bullet sent Ayres rolling but, strange enough, it didn't look like a death shot to me, and it wasn't, but again the blood ran like a hog-stickin', sickening.

Now Bob and Emmett couldn't see Grat and the others and possibly got the notion they had made the alley and the horses, because that's the way they went. But when they got there they knew the truth. Nobody had bothered to stampede the horses, of course, since nobody was thinkin' of anything except the shootin' and killin', but Grat and the others were not in sight. So Bob and Emmett went back to the fight. They could have rode out with twenty thousand dollars. If Grat had not been missin' they probably would, the way they had always short-carded the other boys and all, but in the end the only thing you could say for them was that they did stick together. They had made their brags about the Daltons, and it was maybe their one strong point that they believed it all. Like in the stories Bob and Emmett clipped from the papers and magazines, they had come to be the close-together brothers they had invented and the reporters had built up so big and wonderful.

Now up front where the shootin' was hot Grat fired another shot and hit one of Isham's clerks, Reynolds, in the foot. Isham drug him into the store. Grat was still lookin' for help—he had so much lead in him he couldn't make it to the alley or anywheres else. But he had the rifle reloaded.

Then I saw John Kloehr. He was away over at Read Brothers store with Carey Seaman the barber and Marshal Charlie Connelly. He had stayed there waitin' a clear chance—he wasn't one to rush in. He was a marksman, and all that wild shootin' disgusted him. Carey Seaman was one of the rifle club and he hung there with Kloehr. The Marshal hadn't even worn his gun; he had to borrow one, which he shouldn't have bothered.

He also had a smart idea, but he didn't carry it out right. He thought about the back alley where the horses were waitin' and thought he ought to take a look and see if he could cut off any escape.

Trouble was, he didn't check out on Grat. He had his back to Grat as he went trottin' along carryin' this old carbine. Grat didn't know him from Adam's ox because everything had to be pretty shadowy right then, the condition he was in. But Grat shot Connelly and killed him on the spot.

They were dyin' all over. Powers was already gone. Dick was in the lumber yard tryin' to find strength to make some kind of getaway. Grat surely had it but was still fightin'— and all the townpeople were scared now, seein' Cubine and Brown and Connelly dead and the other wounded. That red blood runnin' from a body will slow down the fight every time. People begin to feel their own mortality, it seems like.

But Kloehr was a different man from the others. He'd always been crazy about guns, and all he had to shoot was targets and some game and no big game at that. Now that it was settled in he started forward, with Seaman behind him. You could see the way he moved, slow and easy, that he was dangerous. I had to keep one eye on him no matter what happened. This was a man I had worked for and I knew him. A silent man with a harsh tongue, a droopy sort of man from his mustache to his saggy pants—now he was like a machine going forward without hurry, cautious but sure. You couldn't miss it—he was a key man, he was the danger.

Bob and Emmett came runnin' up when they saw Grat. They got on each side of him. He couldn't say much because of a wound in his throat, but Bob was talkin' as always and I knew he had to be tellin' that the Daltons could whip the whole town, the whole State of Kansas. That was Bob's way, and to the end he wouldn't know any other.

All of a sudden I saw that Bill Powers had moved. When Bob and Emmett and Grat all began shootin' he had crawled to the alley. How he did it I'll never guess, because he was a dead man when he first fell in the street, but he got onto a horse. And here came Dick Broadwell from the lumber yard. The town was shootin' at the Dalton brothers and the other two were tryin' to make a getaway.

Carey Seaman saw Powers first. He nailed him in the back. Bill fell down off the saddle and now it was really the end of him, his nice new clothing all full of dust and dirt and blood. But Dick hung low on the horse's neck, and damn if he didn't get clear out of Coffeyville. I think Seaman or Kloehr shot him once more as he went, through. It looked that way from where I was.

I could see that Emmett still clung to his wheat sack full of loot and that Bob was sharpshootin' here and there, nothing wild like the others. He almost got Frank Benson and a couple others, but where they were makin' their stand he didn't have a good look at the town, sort of out of direct range. This was savin' them for now, but Bob was for gettin' in his licks. He wasn't thinkin' of runnin' away now, not with Grat bad hurt. He had to make his fight. And Emmett never would do anything exceptin' what Bob did or what Bob told him to do. So there they were, fightin' the entire town of Coffeyville with no more chance than a tissue-paper cat in hell.

I still think at that minute they could've got away if they would leave Grat. Anybody could see Grat wasn't goin' to make it—he was goin' on pure instinct and guts, he was pourin' out blood. The horses were unhurt. Powers and Broadwell had got to them and Bob and Emmett could have done the same and taken the twenty thousand dollars and maybe bought some freedom for a while. Maybe they even could have got Flo and Julia and made it to Mexico. There was always a way when you had that much cash in those days. But they wanted to fight. I've often wondered if maybe the fight and all that wasn't more to them than the money—they never made any real money, never had a big hit until that day in Coffeyville. Maybe that was the trouble with the Daltons, maybe they did believe the legend. If so, they chose a poor time to prove themselves.

Because there was Kloehr and Carey Seaman, that nobody had ever thought much about—a little barber who wore his mustache like Kloehr and all and was just a character of no importance whatsoever. But I guess he had been told what to do and had been practicin' with that rifle real faithful along with the other members of the club. They kept comin'.

Then Bob had to see it all. He moved out of the shelter of the barn and tried to get a look for a target. Seaman shot him in the shoulder.

Bob went staggerin' back. He almost dropped his Winchester, then managed to get hold of it. He looked completely shocked, like this couldn't happen to him—he had never been hit before and it just couldn't happen. He sat down a minute as though to think it over, and Emmett started toward him, and Grat kept mumblin' and shootin' and not hittin' anything or anybody.

Then Kloehr made his move behind a fence. He was stalkin' like a wild-game hunter. I sat up, and if anybody had looked my way I was skylined for fair and would've probably been shot for another member of the gang, the way people was carryin' on and pottin' at everything. I almost pulled my own revolver. It was strange—it didn't seem right, Bob settin' there and tryin' to figure out what had happened and not seein' Kloehr behind the fence. He was a settin' duck if ever there was one.

Kloehr came closer and closer. When he popped up his head he was close enough, believe me. He took a careful aim. It was his luck that Emmett was payin' attention to Bob and not to the fence, or he would have had it right then. As it was, he was steady as though he was in a match for turkeys out on the Kansas flats. He laid that muzzle right on Bob and pulled the trigger.

The bullet hit Bob in the chest. Again, it was like someone had plunked him with a rock and raised dust from his coat. Bob went back, back, back. Kloehr was close enough that the bullet had terrific impact, and Bob just seemed to shrink down, to become small inside his clothing.

That brought Grat up somehow or other. He began to stumble toward the horses, blind, not knowin' from Dixie what he was doin'. Kloehr just pumped in a fresh cartridge and moved his rifle muzzle. He took a lot of time once more. He must've been enjoyin' it. He shot Grat in the throat. The biggest and oldest Dalton went down with his back broken. That was the end of him, even Emmett could see that, even in the terrible position Emmett was now in.

Emmett held onto the sack. He ran, ziggin' and zaggin' down the alley toward the horses. He was young and quick and he made it, swingin' up the sack to the saddle. Now they were all comin', Kloehr and Seaman in the lead. They kept pumpin' shots but it had to be Kloehr that hit Emmett, him or Seaman, one shot in the right shoulder, the other in the hip.

Everybody thought Emmett would still make a run for it. Some went for horses. Others shot down the horses in the alley, killin' them all but the one Emmett was ridin'. There was more hullabaloo and howlin' and yellin' than ever. Emmett boarded his horse and Kloehr missed for the first time, tryin' to make the kill, shootin' for the head instead of the body, or for the horse. Still, Emmett was bleedin' too, and now all the Daltons had been shot that day.

I couldn't help thinkin' how Emmett had always been kindly toward me right from the start, how we were the youngest of the bunch and how he had been about Julia, seldom going to other women and then only to show he wasn't chicken, and how he could cook so good and liked to do it and to keep things neat and clean. He was a big talker like all the Daltons and all that, but I found now that I had always liked him. I had not liked the rest of them much, maybe not at all, but Emmett was different. I was wishin' real hard he would make it out of that alley and away.

And then Emmett did not ride out. He pointed his horse's head at Bob. He came ridin' down that alley and leaned over like some rodeo rider, as if he could pull his brother up into the saddle and carry him off and away from all the bloodthirsty people who were pourin' bullets at them.

It was another dumb Dalton move. It didn't make any sense. Bob was already good as dead; he had no way to get up behind Emmett. Grat was dead. There wasn't any use in it any way you looked at it. But there was simple young Emmett, just about twenty years of age, and he was doin' what nobody in the James-Younger bunch did at North-field—he was tryin' to rescue a brother. And if Grat was brave and Bob didn't know fear, then all I got to say is Emmett was willin' to give up more'n either of them and a better man I haven't knowed since October 5th, 18 and 92.

And it was Carey Seaman who walked up with a shotgun and blasted Emmett right out of the saddle so that he fell in the alley along with Bob and Grat. The little barber beat Kloehr to it, and I don't believe the liveryman ever did forgive Carey for not lettin' him make it a clean sweep of the Dalton brothers.

I was sick, then. There wasn't much in my belly to throw up but I retched on that perch with my head down and my hands covering my eyes. Down below there was a sort of awful silence, then a bunch of Indian-like hootin' and hollerin' that they had got the Daltons. They drug them to Union Street and stretched them out, and some people went after Broadwell.

The rest is well known, you could look it up. They found Dick all right, dead beside his horse. They put him with the others and propped up their heads and found that when they lifted Grat's arm blood came out of his mouth. And some thought that was very funny and kept doin' it, and it was a wonder how much blood there was in the biggest Dalton. You can't hardly blame the people of Coffeyville—there ain't any saints, and they had wiped out the bad bunch.

They found Emmett still alive, and then a lot of people wanted to string him up. John Kloehr and Carey Seaman and others, they had done their jobs and they got in there and stopped Judge Lynch dead. They could shoot folks but they wasn't for a rope finish, and all credit to them.

The banks found all the money—all but twenty-one dollars and some cents, which somebody had no doubt stole.

There was plenty of kids around to grab what was on the ground or in a dead man's pockets. Kids was always broke and wantin' a dollar.

I came down off the roof durin' all this. I saw the photographer—I forgot his name—takin' pictures of the dead as they lay against the wall with their heads propped, not lookin' like Grat and Bob and Dick and Bill but like any other deaders, their clothes all tore and dirty and their boots off, just pitiful. Nobody noticed me. There was too much goin' on, the doctors sayin' Emmett didn't have a chance, but some sayin' he did and all that.

And then I was hungry. I went into the nearest grocery store and bought some stuff and ate it, I couldn't tell you what. It didn't even strike me odd that I was hungry. The weakness had me so that I just was forced to eat.

And then there wasn't a damn thing to do. I didn't even speak to anybody in town. All that millin' around and everything, it didn't seem to mean anything to me. Not that I felt any real, gripin', down-deep grief. The boys had done what they did and they had died game, and Emmett had showed them something. There was nothin' I could do for him or for anybody else in Kansas. I just got back to the sorrel and fed him out of Kloehr's stable and thought a few minutes. Then I got on the horse and just rode out of town to the west. I went slow and easy, a farmer boy in a linsey-woolsey hat, ploddin' along. But when I knew I was clear I took it for Oklahoma, and westward toward Woodward.

♘

SHE KNEW WHEN I GOT THERE, OF COURSE. The news had flown all over the country. She knew most of it. Someone,

I guess it was Bill Dalton, had sent her the Coffeyville *Journal*, which had the story fairly right. Bill had taken care of the burials, and he rode with Emmett to prison after they persuaded Emmett to plead guilty to a killin' which Bob had done in Coffeyville, and he got off with life.

Bill, he came back and was finished in politics and business and all, and he joined Bill Doolin and they were pretty smart for a while and stole a few dollars and then they got it, like all the rest of them. Flo, she never saw them again, so that part was ended.

Flo wanted to know about Emmett and I told her it was true, even his enemies agreed he had tried to save Bob. We was in the barn—me and Flo were together in more barns. First and last, it was like we belonged there.

She said, "So it's over. Over and done with."

"They shouldn't have tried Coffeyville."

"No. You were awful smart the way you got out of it."

"I didn't feel so smart when they were makin' their fight. I tell you, Flo, I almost joined 'em."

"But you didn't. You're no outlaw. I got you into it all. Now what?"

"Why, just as I said before. You and me, we go west where nobody knows us. I already got me a new name. Timothy Older. You see? Not Younger. Older."

"Yes. You're a year older. And I'm thirty years older. I don't want to hurt you any more."

I said, "You never hurt me. You learned me what I know—all of it. This here money I got, it's part yours. Fact is, I'd just as soon you carried it as we go."

"No," she said. "You're the man. Why, you even look like a grown man, twenty-one at least."

"Well, when do we start?"

"Tomorrow, then?"

"Right now, for all of me."

She said slow-like, "I'm packed. No matter whether you came back, I was going. I've got a carriage and a horse, a chestnut that'll match your sorrel. If you could manage them in harness maybe we could leave."

I said, "It'll take a little time about the harness, but that I can do better than anything."

She said, "The harness is up in the loft. I'll show you." She went up the ladder ahead of me. She wasn't wearing anything under the skirt and petticoat. That was Flo all over again. She could've sent me up to get the harness by myself. But she had put the Daltons right out of her life before I ever got there to Woodward, and she never again spoke of them, not once. She had a real knack of never lookin' back over her shoulder, always lookin' ahead.

After we got through in the hayloft, which was a couple of hours, since neither of us had had none in some time, she went to the house and I managed the horses. I talked to them mostly. The sorrel knew me and he didn't like this new thing, but he went along. It's just the way you do it, and there would be some trouble on the way but I knew I could manage it. The chestnut was easier to handle, and maybe it had been driven before. I didn't know where Flo had got it, and of course nobody was goin' to explain to us about it because I was certain the owner didn't know where it had gone. Flo never was one to buy a horse.

She was ready in no time at all. She never did have any truck much with her folks, as I have said. We got into the carriage, which was a two-seater and a very well built one,

171

and we headed west. Flo had a map, so I reckon she had figured I would be back. You never could really figure her out, but that much I guessed and thought I was right. No kid in my position who was in his right mind would've failed to show up and travel cross country with Flo Quick and a beltful of money and plenty of time, more time the farther we got away from the Border States and the Territory.

We just moseyed along from town to town. It wasn't like the old days of the trails west. Towns was connected by roads, which the farmers used to transport their produce and the like. But when you got into cattle country it wasn't so good, and finally we sold the team and the carriage and took the train for Denver. I didn't know why she wanted to go there, but she was always readin' the newspapers and she often kept her notions to herself.

Seemed to me we wasn't spendin' much, and like any kid I thought my money'd last forever. But it got more expensive in the far west. Neither of us drank liquor, me because I needed all my strength to keep up with her in the bed and her because she never did take more'n one or two—reckon she bought more booze than any woman her age in the country, but it all went to the Daltons. But the food got to where it was a dollar for a meal which you could get for twenty cents in Coffeyville, and not near as good, neither.

So in Denver is where she changed her name. She took on a whole new way. She spent money on an outfit which made her look like a queen—some fancy clothes, believe me. She made me dress up like a dude. Then we went to this gamblin' house which was also a whorehouse run by a feller name of McQueen or McKeen or somethin'. I was scared for a minute that Flo was goin' to apply for a job, but she merely took our money and went to a big round wheel, which she said was a roulette wheel and which I had never seen one like it before. And she began to bet our money.

Now that scared me. She sure didn't know a hell of a lot more'n me about this wheel thing. She'd never had any chance to learn about it. But there she was puttin' down money on colors, either black or red. And she won.

Then she pushed a stack of chips on a number. It come up the way she played it. They give her a stack of gold coins that would stagger a blind man.

I was standin' back, lookin' at all the gaslights and the ladies with lowcut dresses and the men in evenin' clothes, which I had never seen before. But I was not asleep. Remember, I was a big kid, very strong and accustomed to hard ways and not about to trust everybody. I seen this McQueen or McKeen give the eye to a big man with a hard face, and the man came and stood beside Flo and when she played another number he played along with her and began talking to her.

Flo gave me a slant-eyed look, which was a signal with us always since we first met and could mean a lot of things, and this time it meant to watch out and don't let on that we knew each other. When she won again after a while she had a sackful—a small fortune to us, more money than the Daltons ever stole in their lives.

The big man said, "Better let me escort you, lady. Denver's a rough town and that kind of money draws crooks like molasses draws flies."

She said, "Why, I do thank you, sir. My name is Mrs. Daniel Doolin."

"I'm Bill Brown," he said. He had a pocketful of coins

too, since he had followed her betting.

The proprietor was watching them. He didn't say anything, but Brown looked at him and he looked back and they were more than acquaintances, it seemed to me. I laid back. I had bought a small, short-barreled .32 revolver when I sold the big hogleg along with the horses and carriage. It was stuck in my pants pocket.

Flo and Brown went out into the street. I followed them, stayin' out of sight as best I could. They came to a street corner on the way to our hotel and he sort of took her arm and led her in the wrong direction. It was dark on the side street.

I came around that corner fast. He had her against a building. She wasn't doing anything, just waiting. I stuck the gun into his side so hard he jumped away, and I almost shot him but Flo spoke in her easy way.

"It's all right, Jim. The gentleman was mistaken. I think you'd better search him."

I jammed him against the building with his back to me. He had a set of brass knucks, a derringer, and a knife on him. He also had those nice gold coins. I took it all. He began cursing.

I said, "Tchk, tchk, with a lady present, too." Then I hit him behind the ear with the muzzle of the revolver. He started to go down and I thought I better make sure, so I hit him again.

Then we went to the hotel and packed and took the night flyer to San Francisco. Flo was laughing all the way. We had a good stake and it had been wonderful taking it away from big city slickers, just a farm girl and boy from the backwoods.

Well, San Francisco was great. Might as well admit, I didn't start right in raisin' fruit and vegetables. What we did was run into a politician who had enough power to protect us in the business. Flo got him as she had so many older men in her time. He was crazy about her, but she always knew things like that wouldn't last. Instead of the house he wanted to give her she took a respectable lookin' house on the edge of the district and began to hire girls.

I worked the place as bouncer and partner for a few years. Me and Flo, we never had a quarrel about anything. She had her ways and I accepted them. She made a lot of money before that miner fella came along—she could've retired when she was not more'n thirty. People liked Flo, and once she settled down she was one wonderful gal.

Never a harsh word between us. And I never bothered with the gals in the house—there was always Flo. She never sold it, neither. I mean, the politician and all that, just like back with Mundy in the old days, to gain some big stake—I don't count that. Flo had to know you and like you, and that's no whore in my way of thinkin'.

Then came the miner fella. He had the same close-set eyes, the hard look, all of it. The spittin' image of Bob Dalton. And there she went, head over heels. Well, I tell you, it did somethin'. Like—what do they say?—it cut a cord.

There come a new gal to the house about then. Pretty as a little speckled hen—young, hardly started. Me, I had seen the miner fella and Flo, and it had done this thing to me, like turned me a-loose. You couldn't make it a hot love affair—nothin' like that. I just kept this little gal for myself. Flo didn't even seem to notice. She was busy.

Finally she did come to noticin' after all. That's when

she come to me with a cash proposition. She bought me out, paid me twice what the house was worth. Said she was goin' to get married, had a buyer for the place. She just laid it all on the line.

We both cried. Like babies. It was strong between us. Age didn't matter, nothin' mattered—it was strong.

So I married the girl—she was my first. She died havin' the third baby. Nice girl. Nothin' in the world wrong with her. But she wasn't Flo. Nobody ever was. Four good gals—I was lucky. None of them like Flo. Not any woman, anywhere, any time.

Now I've outlasted 'em all. And I don't regret none of it. If I did, I'd be dead by now, no doubt. I got today. I wake up, and it takes me some time to believe it, and then my people take care of me and I enjoy what I can eat and I enjoy my wine. I remember.

Flo was the best woman ever lived.

Center Point Publishing
600 Brooks Road • PO Box 1
Thorndike ME 04986-0001 USA

(207) 568-3717

US & Canada:
1 800 929-9108

MG
3/06

ML   8/05